KU-365-135

UNDYING LOVE

Recent Titles by Margaret Pemberton from Severn House

THE FAR MORNING

THE FORGET-ME-NOT BRIDE

THE GIRL WHO KNEW TOO MUCH

THE LAST LETTER

MOONFLOWER MADNESS

TAPESTRY OF FEAR

VILLA D'ESTE

YORKSHIRE ROSE

UNDYING LOVE

Margaret Pemberton

This title first published in Great Britain 1999 by
SEVERN HOUSE PUBLISHERS LTD of
9–15 High Street, Sutton, Surrey SM1 1DF.
Previously published in paperback format only
in Great Britain in 1982 under the title *Forever*.
This title first published in the U.S.A. 1999 by
SEVERN HOUSE PUBLISHERS INC of
595 Madison Avenue, New York, N.Y. 10022.

Copyright © 1982, 1999 by Margaret Pemberton.

All rights reserved.
The moral right of the author has been asserted.

British Library Cataloguing in Publication Data

Pemberton, Margaret
    Undying Love
    1.   Love stories
    I.   Title
    823.9'14 [F]

    ISBN 0 7278 5453 4

684006
MORAY COUNCIL
Department of Technical
& Leisure Services
F

For Josephine Richardson

All situations in this publication are fictitious and
any resemblance to living persons is purely coincidental.

Printed and bound in Great Britain by
MPG Books Ltd, Bodmin, Cornwall.

PROLOGUE

It was night: the hot, sweating and airless night of the deep South. The two girls crouched in the dense undergrowth, the hems of their long skirts wet with mud, foetid with rotting vegetation. They had long since regretted their high-spirited impulse. Now, terrified that movement would lead to discovery, they clung together, their eyes widening and their horror mounting as they witnessed the spectacle taking place in the forest clearing only yards before them.

It was well known in the New Orleans of the early nineteen-hundreds that voodoo rites were rife in the bayous. Sluggish, numberless tributaries of the great Mississippi, the bayous laced the tropical surroundings of the city; were rarely visited places where gigantic trees loomed from stagnant water, their branches draped with Spanish moss, their dense canopy of leaves allowing little light to penetrate.

The bayous were the home of alligators: of eagles: of spiders as big as a man's hand, and of the *voodooiennes*, the Africans who had long lived in New Orleans but had never forgotten their ancient rites.

Seventeen-year-old Leila Derbigny had long suspected that her own maid, Louella, was an initiate into ceremonies that were only whispered about. On certain nights she had seen Louella slip from the servant's quarters and then speedily run away from Sans Souci, the Derbigny plantation house, and into the banana groves beyond.

Whenever Leila questioned her the next day, Louella's

black face would be impassive. A year older than Leila, her eyes were centuries old.

'No, Miss Leila. I ain't been nowhere and don't you go telling your Pa I has been,' she would say, brushing Leila's hair vigorously.

Leila never had. If her father had even the least suspicion that Leila was a participant in the rites he and every other worthy citizen pretended did not exist, she would be immediately dismissed: and Leila was fond of Louella.

Tonight, however, she had been determined to discover the truth of Louella's night-time escapades. Her closest friend, Chantel Gallière, was staying at Sans Souci and Leila had dragged her reluctantly with her in Louella's wake.

At first the way had been easy. The white *tignon* that Louella wore around her dark springy curls guided them like a bobbing lantern. They waited beneath the front gallery until Louella disappeared into the banana grove and then, picking up their skirts, ran in their satin slippered feet across the vastness of Sans Souci's smooth lawns and into the wilderness beyond.

Within minutes Chantel was regretting the escapade. The low flounces of her gown caught on briars and brambles. Her lightly shod feet hurt as they tripped on rocks of petrified palm. The humidity of the tropical night was viscous in its intensity and the thin muslin of her bodice clung to her sweat-soaked skin.

'Let's go back, Leila. We can't possibly keep up with her.'

Leila pulled impatiently at her friend's hand. 'They can't be meeting that far away. Perhaps just beyond the banana grove. Come on, Chantel. We might never have another chance.'

The banana fronds hung listlessly above their heads, their knife-blade edges menacing in the darkness. Chantel had no desire to return through the banana grove by herself. Reluctantly she followed as Leila quickened her pace. The banana grove was left behind. Ahead of them loomed the infinite blackness of oak and cypress. A mosquito circled Chantel's head and she struck out at it before it could land on her shoulders or arms and draw blood.

'Ssssh,' Leila hissed. 'She'll hear us.'

Chantel doubted it. The forest was alive with noise. Insects whirred incessantly. Nameless creatures scurried in the dense undergrowth. Ivy hung in heavy drifts from the gigantic branches above them, catching in her hair, brushing terrifyingly across her face. She choked back a sob. She should never have come. Her dress was torn and ruined. Her pretty pumps were saturated from the increasingly marshy ground. She wanted to be back in the safety of her big soft bed. To hear the comforting movements of servants. To see the reassuring glow of lamplight.

'It can't be much further,' Leila panted encouragingly, disentangling her skirt from a riot of dully gleaming honeysuckle.

'I'm scared, Leila. I want to go home.'

'We can't,' Leila said, suppressing a note of panic in her voice. 'We would never find our way back alone. We must keep following Louella.'

Tears sparkled in Chantel's violet-blue eyes. The bayou stank. The forest pressed in on them malignantly. The night pulsed with heat and the sound of cicadas and then with a sound that sent undiluted fear rippling down her spine. The sound of drums.

'Let's stay here, Leila,' she pleaded. 'Don't let's go any farther.'

Leila shook her head vehemently. She had come this far. She was going to complete what she had set out to do.

The drum-beats grew louder. There came the sound of

tambourines; the rattle of the bones the Black people used in their music. Hardly daring to breathe, Leila inched forward cautiously, crouching low in the lush foliage, tentatively moving overhanging creepers to one side so that they might see.

An oasis of ground was bereft of trees. A large circle of flickering candles illuminated the bodies of fifty or sixty Black people and a handful of *hommes de couleur*. Men neither White nor Black. As the drums increased their rhythm the men and women only yards before them began to dance. Leila could see Louella's white *tignon* flash and whirl, could see that the normally expressionless eyes were brilliant with animation. The dancing grew wilder, terrible in its intensity. This was not the dancing that took place in the Quarter; in the Place Congo. This was something they had never witnessed before. A fevered savagery that held them motionless in terror.

Leila's fingers clutched at Chantel's arm, her breath hoarse in her throat.

'Can you see? There, behind the drums?'

Chantel's heart leapt and then seemed to cease to beat. Beyond the frenzied dancers, dreadful in the candlelight, rose a makeshift altar. Above it two hideous drawings hung suspended. One a depiction of a contorted snake. The other a human heart. Before it were set out a chalice and a prayer-book. And on it was a human body.

'Blessed Mary,' Chantel sobbed, crossing herself, her nails digging so deeply into her palms that they broke the flesh.

'It's a corpse, Chantel. It isn't alive. Look. See how rigid it is.'

Chantel refused to look. She was uncaring as to whether the body was alive or dead. She wanted only to escape from the nightmare around her. To be back at Sans Souci or, better still, to be once more in her own home in the Vieux

Carré. To hear the familiar sound of her father climbing the stairs to his room. To hear the large grandfather clock ticking on the stairway.

The drum-beats ceased. The dancers halted. In front of them an enormous, splendidly robed figure stood commandingly, arms held high.

'It's Valère,' Leila whispered incredulously. Valère. The bald-headed Haitian who served so respectfully in the Gallière household.

Disbelievingly Chantel lifted her head. Her father's servant was hardly recognizable. His nostrils flared. His eyes blazed. He struck terror to the very root of her soul. Her trembling hands found the rosary beads in the pocket of her skirt. Urgently she began to pass them through her shaking fingers.

Valère was chanting prayers. Prayers she had never heard before. Prayers that were not Catholic. Prayers invoking the gods of Africa.

She had to fight to be able to breathe. The pain in her chest was crippling. The blood surged in her ears. Why had they come? Why had they been so foolish?

Majestically Valère moved towards the corpse. Chantel tried to tear her eyes away and found that she could not. Slowly the Haitian circled the lifeless body on the altar and then, in ritualistic grandeur he took a glinting knife and poised it above the corpse's head.

Chantel clenched a fist to her mouth, convinced that she was about to witness a decapitation. The knife arched and the head remained intact. Only hair was shorn, held aloft and then placed in an earthenware jar for all to see. Body hair, too, was removed, and then nails from hands and feet.

'I'm going to be sick,' Chantel sobbed.

'*Be quiet!*' Leila's grasp on her wrist was like a vice.

A chicken was passed to and fro above the corpse and then several feathers plucked and added to the abomination in the jar. Held high for all to see, the jar was sealed. Leila breathed a sigh of relief.

'Well, if that's all. . .' she whispered, grateful to be spared the sight of blood.

To their mystification, Valère then placed the sealed jar high in the boughs of a large oak on the far edge of the clearing.

'Childs play,' Leila said, relieved it wasn't an execution.

Valère then returned to the corpse and marked a cross on its forehead with powder. Then, slowly and ceremoniously, he removed the shoes, turned the pockets of its jacket inside out, and then let out a wild whoop as the drums began once more to pound and the inexplicable performance was completed.

'Let's go!' Chantel cried, pulling herself free of Leila's grasp.

'We'll never find our way back unless we follow Louella.'

'I don't care! I don't care what happens, but I'm not staying here any longer! Not for another minute!'

She scrambled to her feet and began to run. Leila cried out, turning to follow her, her dress impaled on thorns.

'Chantel!'

The drumbeats ceased instantly. There were shouts of alarm: the pounding of running feet.

'*Chantel!*' Desperately Leila pulled herself free and ran but there could be no escape. Chantel was only yards ahead of her. They were seized almost simultaneously.

For the rest of her long life Leila remained convinced that only Louella's intervention saved them from death.

They were dragged down into the clearing, held before Valère, surrounded by shouting, frenzied figures.

'Loa,' Leila heard Louella saying fervently. 'The brides of Loa can never tell.'

It seemed to Leila that an almost imperceptible smile crossed the face of the man who by day served Chantel's father so dutifully. A smile of pure evil. He nodded aquiescence to Louella and Louella hurried to their side as they were hauled to a spot far from the altar.

'What is happening? What will they do to us?' Leila asked in terror.

Louella's eyes held hers. No longer maid but mistress. 'Valère will allow you to become brides of a Loa. As such, he knows you will never talk of what you have seen – or the Loa will exact vengeance.'

'Loa?' Leila felt as if she were falling into a bottomless pit. Were they to be married to one of the dancing Africans?

'A Loa is a god,' Louella said calmly. 'Many women choose to be a god's wife for the benefits he bestows upon them. All through your life, on the first night of the week and on the last, you will sleep alone. Those nights are to be dedicated to Loa. To sleep with your earthly husband on such a night would be to commit adultery and offend the god. Whatever you do, Miss Leila, never offend your god husband. To do so will be to bring down his vengeance on you and your children and your children's children.'

Leila suppressed a sob of relief. They were not to be killed. They were simply to take part in a ridiculous ceremony and then be set free.

'Why did Valère remove the hair and nails from the corpse?' she asked curiously.

Louella bent close to her, her face only inches from Leila's, her voice low.

'Valère is a *hungan*. A priest of voodoo. A man of great power. He wants possession over the spirit of the dead man. The hair and nails contain the soul. Whoever possesses them

11

possesses power over the person from whom they have been taken.'

Leila laughed nervously. 'Why should Valère want power over a man who is dead?'

Louella looked at her strangely. 'There is much you do not know, Miss Leila. Much that you would not believe. The dead can walk. That is why the shoes were removed. So that he can walk quietly.'

'And his pockets?'

'His pockets were emptied to ensure he has nothing with him that can give him power over those he has left behind.' Louella's name was called and she touched Leila's hand briefly. 'Do exactly as you are told and you will be safe.'

As she moved away towards Valère, Leila turned to Chantel.

'There's no need to be afraid, Chantel. You heard what Louella said. It's all a lot of silly mumbo-jumbo.'

Her words of comfort went unheard. Chantel's fear had rendered her almost senseless.

Minutes later Valère was ready to perform the ceremony. Chantel was supported before the altar by strong black arms; Leila defiantly stood alone. Dresses of white were sprinkled with water from the chalice and slipped over their bedraggled gowns. There were prayers and intonations. Proxy husbands stood at their sides and a mockery of a wedding ceremony was endured. Two serpent rings were slipped on each girl's wedding finger. One her own ring, one the ring of her god husband.

They were now the brides of Loa. Participants in a voodoo ritual of which they would never be able to speak.

The Haitian grinned broadly, his huge bald head gleaming in the candlelight. The drums and dancing began again. Revolting liquor was pressed on the girls and they had no option but to drink.

12

The last thing Leila remembered was Louella's face, bending and receding above hers. And Chantel's whimper. That was to remain with her always. The terrified whimpering of Chantel Gallière as she lay on the beaten earth, white skirts billowing around her, her rosary clutched tightly in the palm of her hand.

CHAPTER ONE

She saw him for the first time when she was sixteen. The party at Belle Fleur, the Jefferson's graceful colonial home on New Orleans' St George Avenue was for Natalie Jefferson's birthday. Augusta Lafayette had no idea how old Natalie Jefferson was. It was Natalie's daughter, Mae, who was her closest friend. But at that moment she had no interest in Mae. Her entire attention was centred on the man who dominated the room with his sexual magnetism.

He was tall, inches over six foot. His shoulders were broad. Beneath the exquisite cut of his tuxedo Augusta could see the muscles of his shoulders ripple. There was nothing clumsy or bear-like in Beauregard Clay's stature. He carried his height and breadth with ease and almost animal-like grace.

Beauregard Clay. She had been familiar with his name for years, but the sophisticated circles Beau Clay moved in were not those of a child. Beau Clay, whose widowed father had repeatedly threatened to disown him. Beau Clay who drank harder, drove faster than any other male in Louisiana. Beau Clay, whose lovers were legion and whose photograph appeared in newspapers from Mexico to Montana.

Around her, waiters moved with champagne: maids with exotic delicacies. New Orleans high society laughed and flirted with feverish gaiety.

Someone touched Augusta's arm and asked her for a dance. She refused without turning to see whom the request had come from. Not taking her eyes from the demonic handsomeness incarnate before her.

15

His hair was blue-black, glossy as a raven's wing, curling low over the collar of his lavishly laced and frilled evening shirt. His skin was olive-toned, the bones of his face almost abrasive in their masculinity. His dark eyes swept the room disinterestedly, and her heart ceased to beat for a second as his gaze slid over her and away.

She knew now why he excited such talk: such gossip. There was a brooding restlessness about him that was palpable: a fearlessness, a daring; an insolence towards life that was almost frightening in its intensity. She wanted to touch him more than she had ever wanted anything before in her life.

Her father's cousin, Tina Lafayette, was approaching him, undeniably chic in a sleek fitting gown of black lace that stopped short just above her pretty knees.

Augusta suddenly felt gauche. Her dress was long, as was the dress of every other woman in the room. Only the delightful Tina could have got away with such a breaking of social rules.

'Gussie, darling!' Her aunt had seen her, was facing her across a vast expanse of polished floor and dancers, Beauregard Clay at her side.

Augusta's heart began to beat in slow, thick strokes. They were walking towards her. A slight smile hovered at the corner of Beau Clay's mouth as Tina laughingly whispered up at him. They were in front of her. Gussie gasped. Felt the blood pound in her ears.

'Gussie, darling,' Tina said, lustrous lashed eyes sparkling, 'do meet the most notorious breaker of hearts New Orleans possesses. Beau Clay.'

Her hand was in his. His touch was like fire: she was aflame, burning with heat and longing.

'Beau, meet my cousin, Gussie Lafayette.'

Did she speak? She couldn't remember. His eyes held her prisoner. The music changed to a slow, slumberous waltz.

'There are the Villeneuves,' Tina was saying. 'I must have a word with them before they get lost in the crush. Do excuse me, darlings.'

They were dancing: his body so close to hers that she could smell his skin and feel his heart's strong beat. His grasp was firm: decisive.

'So you're little Gussie Lafayette?'

His voice was deep, rich-timbred, a lazy Southern drawl that sent her spine tingling.

She raised her head to his: his eyes were amused, slanting under winged brows.

'Augusta Lafayette,' she corrected, holding his gaze challengingly. 'I'm not a child, Mr Clay.'

Beau threw back his head and laughed and around the crowded room eyes turned in their direction. Red-lacquered nails tightened jealously on the stems of champagne glasses. Fathers frowned, glad the girl was not their daughter. Bradley Hampton, who had asked Gussie for a dance and been so summarily refused, helped himself to a large glass of rum punch, his young jaw hardening, a nerve throbbing at his temple.

'You're certainly not,' Beau said, black eyes gleaming.

She was a beauty all right. Hair pale-gold and water-straight, hanging in a silky sheen to her waist: eyes violet-dark, with something in their depths that told him she would be worth paying attention to in a year or two.

Above her head, his eyes met Tina Lafayette's and his expression turned to one of heat. Tina Lafayette was thirty-two, five years his senior. But she was a woman in every sense of the word – mature, sensual, and with a sexual appetite that nearly matched his own. The dance had ended.

17

White teeth were flashing in a smile. He was moving away from Augusta.

'No,' Gussie cried, stretching out a restraining hand.

Her plea was lost as the sound of jazz filled the room. Her desperate fingers caught only air. She was hemmed in on all sides by pulsating, gyrating bodies. Beyond them she could see his dark head, see her aunt's pretty blonde curls, and then they were gone.

She moved dazedly to the side of the vast room and sat down on a gilt and velvet chair.

'Beau Clay?' Mae asked in wonderment as they sat drinking Coke by the side of the Lafayette pool. 'You can't be serious?'

Gussie's fingers tightened over the cane arm of her sun-lounger. 'I am, Mae. I'm going to marry Beau Clay. Just you see if I don't.'

'But he's *old*,' Mae protested. 'Twenty-seven or twenty-eight. Besides, his girlfriends are all models or film stars. There was a photograph of him in last week's *States Item* with Zizi Romaine, the star of *Class*.'

Augusta's thickly-lashed eyes narrowed. 'I'm going to marry him, Mae. Nothing on this earth is going to stop me.'

Mae sighed and sipped her Coke. 'There's Bradley Hampton,' she said. 'He's always asking you for a date.'

'Bradley Hampton is a kid.'

'Bradley Hampton is nineteen and was the finest athlete of his grade: or any other for as long as anyone can remember. And his father is the richest man in New Orleans.' She didn't add that his thatch of curly hair and arresting blue eyes also made him the handsomest boy in town. If Gussie couldn't see that for herself, she had no intention of pointing it out. She had ideas herself where Bradley Hampton was concerned.

Gussie rose restlessly and crossed to the pool bar. She mixed herself a forbidden Cuba Libre. What if he never paid attention to her again? What if he married one of his sleek, long-legged beauties? The breath was so tight in her chest it was a physical pain. He *had* to notice her. He *had* to.

Mae, sensing that her presence was no longer desired, slipped her sun dress over her bikini and said, 'I'm going downtown. Are you coming?'

'No.' Moodily Gussie stared into the depths of her drink, her cascading hair obscuring her face. 'See you later, Mae.'

Mae sighed. There had always been something a little strange about Gussie. 'Intense' was the word she had heard her mother use. This sudden infatuation with Beau Clay certainly didn't help.

Gussie returned to the pool with her drink, glad of her own company. Since meeting Beau she had no thought or time for anybody else. She narrowed her eyes against the glare of the sun.

Beau Clay. Beauregard Clay. Augusta Clay. Gussie Clay. Beau and Gussie Clay. Beauregard and Augusta Clay. The names were etched in fire in her brain. If only – if only . . .

If Mae had hoped that Gussie's infatuation was a momentary phase, she was soon disillusioned. All through the following year Gussie's obsession grew. A Lafayette, with her stunning looks and impeccable background, she could have had her pick of the young bloods continually seeking the pleasure of having her on their arm. Nevertheless, Gussie rejected them all. They were not worth her while. They were not Beau Clay.

Mae had tried to reason with her. Beauregard Clay would never look in the direction of a girl as young and innocent as Augusta. His conquests were all women of the world. His tastes did not run to the virginal, even if the virgin was a Lafayette and daughter of one of New Orleans' oldest families. Lafayettes had been prominent citizens in the 1720s when the fleur-de-lis had flown over the city. Beau was uncaring of the family history Charles Lafayette was so proud of.

Judge Matthias Clay, his father, had fondly hoped that Beau would follow in his older brother's footsteps – a glittering college record: a brilliant marriage: a career to add lustre to the name of Clay. But Beau had shown total disregard for his father's wishes. At first, New Orleans society had condoned Beau's scandalous behaviour, his money, charm and devastating good looks strong ameliorating factors. Yet not even the Clay name and wealth could shield Beau from the eventual disapproval of New Orleans society. Husbands cast suspicious looks at their wives whenever Beau Clay entered the same room. There wasn't a woman in New Orleans who wasn't aware of his negligent sexuality.

The young ones yearned hopefully, the middle-aged ones longed vainly, the elderly ones sighed sadly. Beau's lovers came from New York. From Los Angeles. From London. From Paris: picked up and dropped with such rapidity that it was rumoured he never even remembered their names.

This was the man Gussie was convinced would one day marry her. The one for whom she scorned all other dates, preferring to remain day after day in the grandeur of St Michel, her father's magnificent home in the Garden District of New Orleans, with no other companion but a maid.

Mae frowned as she regarded her friend sitting broodingly on the porch swing. She had failed to stop Gussie's obsession, and Gussie's behaviour had not gone unnoticed elsewhere. She had overheard her own mother saying tartly that Gussie was no different from her grandmother Gallière.

20

Their grandmothers. Why was it that no one would ever talk about their grandmothers? Mae's mother could not be coaxed, would change the subject the moment Mae entered the room. All that Mae knew about her own grandmother was that she lived the life of a recluse in a crumbling, tumble-down plantation deep in the bayous in Cajun country. Mae had heard it said that Leila Derbigny had been a beauty in her time and that Henry Jefferson had been fortunate in winning her for a bride. Mae still thought her grandmother beautiful in her grandmother's own strange and eccentric way. But visits to her were discouraged – had always been discouraged. As for Augusta's grandmother, she was never spoken of. Not even in the Lafayette household. All that Gussie herself knew was that, within a year of Chantel marrying Julius Lafayette and then giving birth to Charles Lafayette, Chantel had committed suicide, drowning herself in one of the deserted, desolate lakes that lay deep in the Louisiana forests.

Had Chantel been mad? Unbalanced? A normal, healthy woman would never have chosen such a death, and Chantel Lafayette had been scarcely a woman. Only twenty when she had waded into the alligator-haunted water, deeper and deeper, her wheat-gold hair fanning around her as she embraced death.

Mae shivered. Was Gussie unbalanced? Certainly her obsession with Beau Clay – nearly a year old now – had become alarming in its fixation.

'Austin Merriweather has asked me to the Carlton dance. I know Bradley wants to take you. Why don't we make a foursome? It would be fun.'

Gussie swung to and fro, fanning her face as the heat throbbed in the air, rising in waves over St Michel's lushly tended lawns.

'If I go to the Carlton dance, I'll go with Beau.'

21

'But Beau isn't even aware of your existence!' Mae cried exasperatedly. 'You're wasting your life, Gussie. Throwing it away on a dream.'

Gussie's eyes sparked fire. 'I'm waiting for my life to begin, Mae! And it will. I'm seventeen now – nearly eighteen. I can go to the same places Beau goes. The same parties. The same clubs. Just another few months and I'll be Mrs Beau Clay. I will. *I will!*' Feverishly she pummelled the cushions on the swing.

Mae stared at her and the nape of her neck prickled. The Gussie before her was not the Gussie she had grown up with. There was nothing more to say. She left awkwardly. She couldn't confide in Austin. She certainly couldn't confide in her mother. Her mother would say Gussie was mad: as Gussie's grandmother had been. She couldn't confide in Gussie's father, Charles Lafayette. If he knew for one second that his daughter was obsessed with Beau Clay, he would send her to Europe and Mae would have lost her best friend.

Miserably she drove her Mercury down St Michel's long drive. She would go and see Eden Alexander. Eden had enough common sense to restore her spirit and put everything into perspective.

Eden regarded Mae with amusement. 'Gussie is no madder than you or me. Let's take some rum over this evening and have a party. Her father is playing bridge with my parents and Mrs James-Stanley. One thing about having no mother is that it makes fun at home easier.'

They laughed.

Gussie's mother had died in childbirth and Gussie had grown up the adored child of her father and had never for a moment missed the presence of a mother. As for Eden and

Mae, although they loved their respective mothers, there were certainly times when they were an inconvenience.

To Mae's relief Gussie was undeniably pleased to see Eden. It wasn't always so easy since Eden's parents were newcomers to New Orleans, French-Canadians who were not of the same social elite as the Jeffersons or the Lafayettes, but who were intent on storming the bastions of the city's rigid society.

'I'm not going out with Don Shreve again,' Eden said, expertly mixing up an exotic rum punch as they sat listening to records in the grandeur of St Michel's main salon. 'He takes liberties I wouldn't allow Burt Reynolds.'

Mae giggled. 'I'd allow Burt Reynolds anything.'

Eden and Gussie laughed. 'Mae Jefferson. You're becoming perfectly immoral.'

'Not with Austin,' Mae said, and the laughter increased.

Austin Merriweather III had many agreeable qualities. He was kind, rich and suitable but he was certainly no sex symbol.

The glasses were handed round. Jazz filled the room, soft and low. 'I don't think I *can* be in love with Austin when I still want to date Bradley Hampton so badly,' Mae said, hugging her knees as they sat companionably on scatter rugs, the highly polished wood floor gleaming in the lamplight.

'I think I'm in love with Dean Kent,' Eden said calmly.

'*Dean Kent!*' Mae nearly choked on her drink and Gussie stared, round-eyed. Dean Kent was a lawyer: a close friend of Eden's father. A suave, sophisticated, handsome man in his late thirties.

'Does your father know?'

'Don't be silly,' Eden said smugly. 'He'd throw a fit.'

'But Dean Kent is *old*,' Mae protested, shock making her unwise. 'He's even older than Beau Clay.'

23

Eden's eyes took on a dreamy expression. 'Now *there's* a man who could tempt me from Dean.'

Mae's eyes swung in Gussie's direction but Gussie was sipping her drink, seemingly undisturbed. Mae relaxed. Gussie was all right. She'd been foolish to imagine otherwise.

'Wouldn't it be marvellous if you could make who you wanted fall in love with you?' Eden said idly, helping herself to more punch. 'Who would I choose? Burt Reynolds? Dean Kent? Beauregard Clay?'

Eden's exotic mixture of rum and curaçao had made Mae light-headed. 'You can if you really want to,' she said suddenly. 'If you really want to bad enough you can make anyone fall in love with you. I saw Bradley last night and I lay awake for hours wondering if I should make him love me. But I don't know whether I want to badly enough. Besides, the thought scares me a little.'

Eden laughed. 'Don't be a goose, Mae. You couldn't make Bradley fall in love with you. He's in love with Gussie.'

'I could make him love me if I wanted to,' Mae repeated stubbornly.

'How?' Eden's voice was amused, but in the glow from the lamps Gussie's eyes had taken on a peculiar light and she had gone very still.

Mae drained her glass and obligingly allowed Eden to refill it. 'My grandmother says it's an old New Orleans tradition that if you want someone to love you forever you need only write his name *backwards* on a piece of paper ... and then eat it!'

Eden laughed delightedly. 'How do you spell Burt Reynolds backwards? I'd just love a six-month *affaire* with that man.'

'It's forever, Eden.'

'Can't it work just for a few weeks?'

'No. It's forever and forever and forever.'

'Then it's no good. I don't want Burt Reynolds forever. I shall want someone else afterwards. I'm growing up an insatiable lady.'

'I want Beauregard Clay forever,' Gussie said suddenly.

The laughter faded. 'Would you do it, Gussie?' Eden asked.

Gussie's eyes were feverish. 'I'm *going* to do it. I'm going to make Beauregard Clay love me forever. Just you see if I don't.'

'It only works on Midsummer's Eve,' Mae said apprehensively. Gussie's eyes gleamed. 'It's Midsummer tomorrow. That's why you remembered it, why you thought of writing Bradley Hampton's name on the paper and eating it. Are you still going to do it?'

'I don't know. I'd *like* to, but I'm scared.'

'Who could be scared of eating a piece of paper?' Eden said affectionately.

'Then you do it as well.'

Eden shrugged. 'There's no one that I want forever. It's too long a time.'

'Not for me,' Gussie said passionately. 'For me, forever won't be long enough!'

'I bet you don't go through with it,' Eden said, replacing Miles Davis with Cleo Laine.

'I shall. Come over tomorrow night and see.'

The instant Mae had spoken Gussie had known that what she had said was true. She had felt the truth deep within her. It had seemed to strike some primeval chord that had previously lain dormant. She had known all along about the Midsummer's Eve ceremony, though no one had told her of it. The knowledge was in her blood and bones. She couldn't wait for Eden and Mae to leave. To run up to her bedroom and savour the excitement rising within her. She sat on the enormous bed, her arms around a carved rosewood post, her cheek pressed close to the wood.

Soon Beau Clay would be hers. She could almost feel the weight of his body forcing hers to be still. His mouth bruising and burning, his hands searching and demanding. With single-minded determination she began to count away the long hours.

Thoughts of Beau Clay had driven all other thoughts from her mind. She woke next day with an exclamation of horror. Tomorrow was not only Midsummer's Day, it was her father's birthday and she had still not brought him a present. A book, she decided as she dressed, ignoring the breakfast tray that had been brought up for her. Something that showed it had been chosen with care. She wriggled her slim hips into a pair of Parisian-cut jeans. She could order one over the telephone and have it delivered, but for the life of her she could not think of a suitable title. She needed to go down to Dolpen II and browse around.

Picking up a slice of toast, she ran lightly down the balustraded stairs and out into the heavy sunshine. Going for the book would help pass the time until evening. She felt sick with excitement. Mae's grandmother was known for her skill in telling the future and there were rumours that she possessed far more sinister talents. It was whispered that she was far too friendly with her Black servants; that she knew secrets of voodoo and witchcraft. Even that she was an initiate. If Leila Jefferson said a man's heart could be bound forever by such a simple ritual, then Augusta believed her.

Augusta parked her Chevrolet in Royal Street and strolled into Dolpen's. She selected a glossy coffee-table book retelling for the hundredth time the Battle of New Orleans. It wasn't a very original present but it was one that would please. There were suitably flattering mentions of the

Lafayettes who had fought alongside General Jackson. How was it, Gussie thought, her arms clasping the book, her eyes taking on their all-too-familiar far-away expression as she left the shop, that in the days of old New Orleans all the men had been so dashing and devil-may-care and now, in the same city, they all seemed so everyday and ordinary. Apart from Beau, of course. Beau still carried a sense of danger and excitement with him wherever he went. He had only to enter a room for the whole atmosphere to become electric.

A dark figure stepped forward and caught hold of her arm. She gasped. For a second she thought it was Beau, for he moved with the same easy strength and confidence, and then disappointment flooded through her.

The hair was nearly as dark but instead of hanging in a glossy sheen, it was coarse and curly, tumbling low over well-marked brows. The laughing eyes held none of the black glitter of Beau's.

'You scared me half to death,' she said bad-temperedly, wrenching her arm away from Bradley's grasp.

He grinned. 'I saved you from disappearing beneath the wheels of a Cadillac.'

There was an ominous roll of thunder and the sun disappeared behind burgeoning black clouds. The first heavy drops of rain spattered on the cover of the book.

'We'd best take cover.' His hand was on her arm again.

She shook it away, saying irritably, 'I *like* rain. I *enjoy* thunder-storms.'

Bradley shrugged. A little rain never hurt anyone. If she didn't mind, he sure as hell didn't.

'Which way are you going?'

She hesitated, looking around her with slight bewilderment. They were in the middle of Jackson Square. The band that had been playing was hurrying for shelter. The pavement artists were rapidly removing their pictures from the railings. With a slight furrowing of his brow Bradley realized that she had not known where she was.

'To my car. I left it near Dolpen's.'

The rain was coming down with a vengeance. The square, full only minutes ago, was now empty. Lightning flashed viciously over the cathedral and the rows of balconied nineteenth-century buildings. Taking her arm for the third time, Bradley led Augusta firmly in the direction of Royal Street. He preferred her like this: bad-tempered, out of breath, her face streaked with rain, her hair falling wildly around her shoulders as she was forced into a run by the rain that bounced off the pavement like bullets. At least she was with him in mind as well as body. Not just lost in some private world of her own.

'Storms suit you,' he said as they raced to the far side of the square.

'You're crazy.' She was panting, her nipples showing clearly beneath the saturated cotton of her T-shirt.

'I know.' His voice caught and deepened. There was a sudden flexing of muscles along his jaw line. Without any warning he halted and swung her round to face him.

'What the— ' she began.

Her breasts were pushed flat against his chest as he caught her to him, silencing her protests with a long, deep kiss. The book scored her ribs so that she wanted to cry out in pain. She let go of it and pummelled clenched fists against his rain-soaked shoulders. His lips were hard and insistent and he had wound one hand in her hair so that she could not twist free.

She struggled vainly, the book slipping and then falling on to the flooded pavement. Finally she tore her mouth from his, her nails scoring deep marks down the side of his face.

'I'll never forgive you for this, Bradley Hampton! Never!

Never! *Never!*' She was gasping for breath, her eyes feral in their fury.

He stared down at her, his face ashen. He had been patient long enough. 'Who is he?' he demanded harshly. 'Who the devil *is* he?'

'*Beauregard Clay!*' She spat the name, stooping down to retrieve the ruined book. '*And he loves me, and he'd kill you if he knew what you had done!*' Sobs rose in her throat. Clutching the book fiercely, she swung away from him, running blindly across the rain-lashed square.

Bradley watched her, his mouth a tight line of pain. Beau Clay. He should have known. Frowning fiercely, he retraced his steps. There were plenty of other girls in New Orleans. He slammed into a phone booth and dialled Mae Jefferson's number.

Augusta was shaking by the time she reached her car. Bradley Hampton had spoiled her entire day. For months she had kept herself as untouched as a nun. All for Beau. Now, on the very eve that her waiting would be over, Bradley Hampton had kissed her with indecent thoroughness and in the middle of Jackson Square.

And her father's birthday present was ruined.

'Damn Bradley Hampton,' she said, crashing through the gears, driving at a speed that was illegal. 'Damn him, damn him, damn him!'

She spent the rest of the day in her room. The book, once it had dried out, had proved to be not so ruined after all. She had written prettily in it and wrapped it with care. Her father was having friends round for a game of cards in the evening. She need make no excuse for avoiding his company. She remained alone all through the long afternoon. Her score of dolls stared steadfastly at her. She rearranged them, adjusting a skirt here, a bow there. They all had old china faces and soft bodies. Each one was older than herself: legacies from her grandmother and her mother. The mother she had never known.

When the sunlight began to change to a soft glow, she bathed in deeply scented water and dressed for the coming ritual in the long, rose-pink gown her Cousin Tina had given her as a present after Tina's last Parisian trip.

Eden arrived first and raised delicate eyebrows. 'My, my, we are taking it seriously, aren't we?'

Gussie's pansy-dark eyes held hers with such intensity that Eden's smile faded.

'It *is* serious, Eden Alexander. If you don't think so, you'd best leave right now.'

'Apologies, apologies,' Eden said, falling on to the lace-covered bed. 'I wonder if Mae is going to go ahead and bind Bradley Hampton to her forever? I shouldn't think he'll be very pleased if she did.'

'I'm not,' Mae said, entering the room nervously. 'And I don't think Gussie should bind Beau to her either.'

'It's only a game,' Eden said lazily, careful that Gussie did not hear her. She sighed and opened a packet of cigarettes. Goddammit. It wasn't as if it would work. It would take more than a chewed-up piece of paper to make a man like Beau Clay take notice of seventeen-year-old Augusta Lafayette. Mae was taking the whole thing too seriously.

Gussie was glad Mae had changed her mind about joining her in the ritual. She wanted to do it alone: without Mae or anyone else taking part. Tonight was special. It was going to alter her whole life. Tonight Beauregard Clay would be hers – forever.

'What do we do now?' Eden asked as the sun sank in a blood-red haze. A strange calm seemed to have settled over Gussie.

'We wait just a little longer. Until it's quite dark.'

Even Eden began to grow nervous as the shadows in the

30

room lengthened and the velvet of dusk turned into the darkness of night. Just when she was about to make her excuses and leave, Gussie rose from the bed and very slowly, almost regally, lit the candles in the candelabras at either side of her dressing-table mirror.

'Oh my,' Mae whispered fretfully, twisting her handkerchief in her hand. 'I wish I'd never suggested this! What if . . .'

'*Shshsh!*' Eden said, gazing wonderingly at the almost ethereal expression on Gussie's face.

Mae shushed, watching unhappily as Gussie sat on her dressing-table stool and began to brush her hair in long rhythmic strokes until it flowed down her back like a web of silk.

Even Eden was subdued. Gussie no longer looked like the girl she knew. She looked almost spectral.

There was a concerted intake of breath as Gussie picked up the silver fountain pen inscribed with her mother's initials and in a strong, firm hand, and without a moment's hesitation, wrote boldly YALC DRAGERUAEB.

'No!' Mae whispered. 'Oh please, no!'

A slight smile curved Gussie's lips. With cool deliberation she put the piece of paper into her mouth and swallowed.

The room erupted around her.

'Upon my life, she's done it!' Eden shouted, leaping from the bed and seizing Augusta's hand. 'Do you think you feel any different? Has it worked?'

Gussie remained seated, staring into the candle-lit mirror, her eyes incandescent.

'I'm sure I felt a cold wind blow through the room when she put the paper in her mouth,' Mae said with a shiver.

Eden hooted with laughter. 'You're scared of your own shadow, Mae.

'Let's have some wine and celebrate.' Eden held a bottle

31

of Chablis triumphantly aloft. 'It's not very chilled, but who cares? Come on, Gussie. Have a drink. You deserve it. Weren't you scared? Not even for a second?'

'*I* was scared all the time,' Mae confessed. 'I didn't dare look into that mirror. Did you see anything in the mirror, Gussie?'

The wine splashed into hastily gathered glasses.

'To Augusta Lafayette,' Eden cried, standing in the centre of Augusta's vast bed and holding her glass high in a toast. 'The girl Beau Clay will love forever!'

'To Gussie!'

Glasses clinked and the colour gradually returned to Mae's cheeks.

'I guess it was all right after all,' she said with a giggle of relief. 'Nothing dreadful happened, did it?'

'It will if we don't leave this very minute,' Eden said, a new inflection in her voice. 'It's five to twelve. If I'm out after midnight again this week my father's going to put some of his threats into action.'

'Mine too,' Mae said, scrambling from the bed.

'Bye, Gussie. It's been fun.'

'Bye.'

'Bye.'

Gussie stood at the head of the stairs, watching them hurry down towards the door where Louis, the Black butler, waited to close it behind her guests. A sliver of light showed beneath the card room door, indicating that her father's card game was still in progress.

With suppressed giggles the girls disappeared into the darkness and towards their cars. Louis closed the door and shook his head in silent reproof.

Augusta let out a deep sigh and turned once more to her candle-lit room. She had done it! She had done it and she knew it had worked. She clapped her hands and whirled joyously around the bed.

The face in the candle-lit mirror had not been hers. It had been Beau's: dark and lean, with mocking eyes, his mouth crooked in the merest hint of a smile.

'Soon, dear love,' she whispered feverishly to herself, pressing her face against the freezing cold of the window pane, staring out into the darkness. 'Soon!'

Somewhere out there was Beau, his heart no longer his own, but hers. She sighed ecstatically. In the next few days New Orleans was going to be rocked on its heels. The notorious Beau Clay would be tamed at last. And by little Gussie Lafayette.

Humming softly to herself, feeling like a bride on her wedding night, she stepped free of her dress and slipped naked between the lace-edged silk sheets. 'Beau Clay,' she murmured, drifting off to sleep. 'Beau Clay ... Beau Clay ... Beau ...'

CHAPTER TWO

Raucous laughter filled the richly ornate room. The house was one that slept by day and came into its own at night. Way beyond the shacks on the outskirts of the city, it was a house unknown to decent people. A house visited only by the disreputable and dissolute. Once it had been the gracious home of a plantation owner. Cypress swamps flanked it on one side, the broad sweep of the Mississippi on the other. It was known to those who frequented it as simply 'The Château'. Two storeys high, embraced on all sides by balconies and Doric columns, it had been built by its original owner with lavish expense and pride. Now the heavy drapes at the tall French casement windows were seldom drawn back. The high-ceilinged rooms were no longer the scenes of elegance and refined entertainment. While the marble mantles and crystal chandeliers remained, the overall effect of the crimson velvet sofas and faded tapestries was one of uncaring shabbiness. Cigarette and cigar ash was dropped indiscriminately, the sweet smell of marijuana and not potpourri pervaded the mirrored rooms.

Outside it was hardly visible from the road. Dense oaks shielded it from view. Riverwards, what had once been carefully tended gardens ran wild with tropical vegetation and a tangle of orange and lemon trees. The Château was as unapproachable as its occupants could wish.

Beauregard Clay laid down his hand of cards and tipped his chair back on two legs against a gold flock-papered wall, surveying the man opposite him through half-closed eyes.

His opponent was an out-of-towner, a Northerner who had already lost twenty thousand dollars in the game that had started only hours earlier. Von Laussat and Shenton Ross, Beau's shadows, sat tensely, well aware that even at this stage, if he lost, Beau could not make true his debt. Judge Clay had issued orders to the bank that no more of Beau's cheques were to be honoured. As the money Beau habitually drew was deposited by the Judge, the bank had nervously acceded to his request. Beau had been indifferent.

The stakes on the table went up by another five thousand dollars. Idly Beau scanned his hand and topped two pairs with a flush.

A girl whose beauty showed her mixed ancestry entered, hips swinging, from a distant smoke-filled room, a bottle of bourbon and a glass in her hand. Beau stretched out a free hand and the Northerner frowned, studying his cards with tense scrutiny. The girl gave a throaty laugh and sat easily on Beau's lap, one arm around his neck, the other pouring bourbon into the glass. Beau drank deeply, aware that the Northerner was carefully calculating the amount of alcohol he consumed. Beau's mouth curved in the semblance of a smile. If the Northerner was hoping that the bourbon would cloud his judgement, he was hoping in vain.

Another hand went down to Beau, and Von and Shenton exchanged triumphant glances. With Beau holding the cards, gambling was a cinch.

By eleven-thirty the Northerner knew the game was lost beyond recovery. Grinding his cigar into the onyx ashtray, he accused Beau of cheating. In three hours he had lost fifty thousand dollars. Beau shrugged nonchalantly, pointing out that the stakes had not been of his calling.

'Bastard! Cardsharp!' the Northerner yelled, sweeping the cards from the table, the inch of liquor remaining in the bottle gurgling to the floor.

With the sigh of a man facing the boring inevitable, Beau pushed the girl unceremoniously from his knee.

'Thieving son-of-a-bitch!'

The table went crashing as the mottle-faced Northerner sprang to his feet and lunged at Beau.

Von folded his arms across his chest and leaned against the wall. He liked to see Beau in action. It was poetry in motion. No matter how beaten and bloody his victim, Beau always emerged unscathed, his expression as confident as ever, his breathing prefectly in control, his clothing barely disarranged. Moving adroitly he side-stepped the vicious punch intended for his face, seized hold of a shoulder carried forward by its own momentum, steadied it and then smashed a clenched fist into a helplessly waiting jaw. The sound of bone against bone made Von wince. The Northerner was on his knees, blood pouring from the follow-up blow Beau had delivered to his nose. Through the mask of blood Von judged that it was broken. He watched with grudging admiration as the man struggled to his feet, arms flailing wildly in Beau's direction.

An expression of distaste flicked across Beau's face. He had no desire to bloody his silk shirt or exquisitely tailored tuxedo. With a swift blow to the stomach he rendered the Northerner senseless. Contemptuously kicking the inert body with the toe of his shoe, he left Von and Shenton to crawl on the floor, scooping up the confetti of one hundred dollar bills, and with an arm around the girl's waist, strolled negligently into a lavishly furnished bedroom.

He stretched out on the bed, his arms locked behind his head, his shirt open to the waist, displaying a mass of tightly curling hair and gold chains.

The girl took her time. She knew Beau's mood and she knew that he was in no hurry. Tonight was going to be good for her as well as for him. With the provocativeness of a professional artist she began to undress, her honey-gold skin glowing satin-soft in the lamplight. Beau watched her with appreciative eyes. It was no wonder the clubs paid her a thousand dollars a week for a ten-minute-a-night spot.

The bed was tented and canopied, mosquito netting looped loosely against the bedposts. Her breasts teased him through their restraining wisp of black lace. His sex throbbed and his eyes darkened. The three-times married, twenty-seven-year-old socialite he had dated in the afternoon had thought herself devastatingly experienced. If he had wanted, Beau could have told her she still had a lot to learn.

Deep in the cypress swamps an owl hooted and there came the screech of a taloned rabbit. He glanced at his watch. It was five to midnight. Afterwards there would be a game of cards until dawn and then he would fly his Cessna to La Jolla and the stunning Californian who had graced the centre spread in last month's *Playboy*.

The girl twirled, discarding the wisp of lace. Beau eased himself up on one elbow, about to reach out for her and then stopped. A pain shot up his arm and into his chest and for one shattering moment he thought he was experiencing a heart attack. He gasped and the girl halted, her fingers hooked into the top of her panties.

'What is it, honey? What's the matter?'

Beau stared at her and through her. Augusta Lafayette. Why the hell was he thinking of Augusta Lafayette at a time like this? The pain receded, leaving a burning sensation, as if he had been scorched.

The panties went the way of the bra and the girl swayed towards him, winding her fingers in his hair, pressing his face against her breasts. Brutally he pushed her away.

Augusta Lafayette. Her face swam before him as if it were in the room. Strange how he had never noticed before how ethereally beautiful she was. Those eyes, velvet-soft, violet-dark. A man could lose himself in such eyes. Drown in them. He felt as if he were drowning now. He wanted to reach out and seize hold of her but all that was before him was a heavily perfumed body that held no allure.

Augusta Lafayette's body held allure in plenty. He remembered holding it at a nameless party, feeling the incredible smallness of her waist, the high pert breasts, the willingness as she had pressed close against him. His head swam. He was aware of the girl's indignant exclamations and was uncaring of them. Why hadn't he stayed with Augusta Lafayette at that party? The answer was swift. He had thought her a child and had treated her as such. He swung his legs off the bed, trying to think clearly. She *was* a child. Sixteen- or seventeen-year-olds held no charms for him. He liked his women experienced. He left the deflowering of virgins to Von, who couldn't get enough of them. As if from a vast distance, he heard a female voice rising higher and higher. He swore savagely. He wanted to think; he wanted to hold on to the vision before him.

Her sun-gold hair was shining like a halo, spreading over her shoulders and down her back to the base of her spine. Hair like silk. Hair to lose himself in. Her lips were parted and smiling invitingly. She was radiant, lit with an inner flame.

He sprang from the bed, grabbing his jacket as he strode from the room.

'Where are you going? What's gotten into you?' the girl asked indignantly, seizing his arm. She was rewarded by a thrust that sent her sprawling to the floor.

'I thought we were having a game of poker?' Shenton said bewilderedly as Beau slammed the door of the bedroom behind him and headed for the marbled entrance hall. 'Your cards are waiting.'

'Another night.'

Shenton shrugged and prepared to follow him. Beau swung round, and at the expression in the black eyes, Shenton faltered.

'I've a visit to make,' Beau said tersely. 'Alone.'

Around the room the kissing and cuddling, the card playing had come to a halt. His friends eyed him nervously. Beau's temper was legendary but it was generally only directed at outsiders; at men like the Northerner. Now, the restraint he usually exercised while in the presence of his friends, was gone. There was a wildness about him that was almost demonic. Pausing only to drain Shenton's glass of brandy, he stalked out of The Château and into the sultry night like a man possessed.

'Should we go after him?' Von asked hesitantly.

Around the room feet shuffled, but no one moved forward.

A car door slammed. There was the sound of an engine being revved viciously.

'Perhaps he's drunk?' Von's girl suggested.

'He's always drunk,' Shenton said curtly, eyeing the empty bottle of bourbon. 'But it doesn't usually take him this way.'

'We'd never catch up with him now,' the son of one of New Orleans' leading citizens said as the sound of the engine faded into the distance.

Shenton still hesitated.

'Aw, come on. It's after midnight. If we're going to play poker, let's play. Beau can look after himself.'

Reluctantly Shenton sat down at one of the tables. He was filled with a sense of unease. Beau's behaviour had been out of character. He had looked like a man demented when he'd stormed out of The Château: a man not in control of himself. Unhappily he picked up the cards that had been dealt Beau

39

and his scalp tightened and prickled. The ace of spades: the card of death.

Beau sped suicidally down a road bounded by cypress swamps and occasional sheets of moonlit water. The urgency he felt inflamed him. He'd wasted weeks, months. He wasn't going to waste another hour. He would break down the door of St Michel if necessary, but he would have Gussie Lafayette. The tyres screeched as he took a corner on two wheels. There would be no need to snatch Gussie from her father's grasp. The doors of St Michel would be open, waiting for him as Gussie would be.

The needle on the speedometer flickered from ninety to a hundred. He could see her face as clearly as if looking at a reflection in a mirror. Her eyes were aglow, her hair cascading down her back, her small rounded breasts rising and falling beneath her rose-pink gown.

She was in candlelight and he felt as if he could almost touch her. The blood coursed through his veins. Augusta Lafayette. Of all the women in the world to fall in love with, he'd fallen for little Gussie Lafayette!

'I'm coming, sweetheart,' he said, his black eyes dancing at the thought of Charles Lafayette's horror, of his father's staggered amazement. 'I'm coming, Gussie, and we'll be together forever! Forever!'

The wheel spun beneath his strong hands, the needle flickering to one hundred and five, one hundred and six. Out of the darkness the giant oak seemed to race down on him. He screamed in protest, raising his arm to shield himself as the car rocketed into the tree and then soared into the air with the momentum, rolling over and over, glass shattering and steel crashing as it somersaulted into the sucking blackness of the swamp.

'If that's for me, tell them I'm out,' Judge Clay growled as the telephone rang insistently.

'Yes, sir.' The maid deposited the fresh coffee on the breakfast table and silenced the offending ringing. She came back into the sun-filled room apprehensively.

'It's the Sheriff for you, Judge. Says it's mighty important.'

'Goddammit, can't a man have breakfast in peace?' Judge Clay slammed down his napkin and stormed to the telephone. Seconds later he was out of the house and heading east.

'Of course, we don't know for certain yet,' Sheriff Surtees said as chains were manacled to the underside of the car, 'but the plates were visible and when I saw the make and that it had been sprayed black with a fancy gold trim . . .'

The Judge wasn't listening. The tree lay across the road, decapitated at its point of impact with the car. The vehicle lay in the swamp, only the wheels and underside exposed. Whoever had been driving was long dead. Some yards away an ambulance waited, but only to serve as a hearse. Around him the rescue services were working smoothly and efficiently. The car was anchored, the crane creaked and the swamp reluctantly released its prize.

If Judge Clay had hoped that his son's car had been driven by one of his wild friends, his hopes were in vain. Beau was at the wheel, rigid in death, his arm still across his face, his neck broken.

'Beauregard Clay's dead!' Eden Alexander's mother said over the phone to her closest friend. 'I heard it from Ellen Surtees.'

'Beau Clay's finally overreached himself,' Jason Shreve Sr said to his wife at lunchtime. 'Drunk out of his skull, I shouldn't wonder.'

'Beauregard's dead,' his brother said tearfully to his wife. 'That was Pa on the phone. A car accident . . .'

'Beau Clay's dead. My, that *is* a tragedy,' Natalie Jefferson said as she supervised lunch. 'He would have settled down in time. Why, what's the matter Mae? You look quite pale. Don't you want another piece of pecan pie?'

'Beau Clay dead?' Charles Lafayette said queryingly to his third client of the morning. 'I can't say I'm surprised. That kind of wildness can only end one way. Still, it's a tragedy. He had promise. I feel for his father. Now, what were you saying about the oil refinery's requirements?'

'Judge Clay's son is dead,' Don Shreve's mother said, wide-eyed, to her husband. 'Hit a tree and died instantly. At least, I *hope* he died instantly. His neck was broken but he could still have been alive, couldn't he? Drowning in that hideous swamp. It makes me quite ill to think of it. Him so handsome, too.'

'Beau's dead,' Augusta's Cousin Tina shrieked, the blood draining from her pretty face as she stared at the ghastly headlines in the paper. 'It can't be true! It can't be! Oh my God! Beau! Beau!'

'I always did say that Beau would come to a bad end,' the town's leading matron said to her sister, helping herself to a glass of sherry and ignoring the fact that it was only four in the afternoon. 'Wild as an unbroken stallion, he was. Why, I remember him flying that plane of his so low it near took the roof off the Shreve's place. And then there was the time with Judge Foster's wife. Never gave a flying damn whether the Judge knew or not. He had the Devil in him all right. My, but his death is going to cause a lot of broken hearts.'

'It's a tragic waste,' Bradley Hampton's father said to the to the head of Nadvasco Oil, removing his glasses. 'Dead at twenty-seven.' He shook his head. 'He had talent for all he

42

was wild. All that young man needed was the steadying influence of a good wife.' He eyed the photograph of his son on his desk speculatively. 'Marriage can settle a boy like nothing else. I know. I married at twenty and never regretted it. I've been thinking lately that Bradley is growing too headstrong for his own good.' He tapped his glasses on the leather surface. Something would have to be done concerning Bradley. He had narrowed his choice of suitable daughters-in-law down to three. There weren't many girls fit for marriage to a Hampton.

'He's dead!' Shenton's mother said to her husband unbelievingly. 'Beauregard is dead!' She stumbled for a chair. 'What if Shenton had been with him? It could have been Shenton at the bottom of that swamp! Oh, I think I'm going to faint. Brandy, somebody, quickly!'

'Lord, Lord, but that boy sure done it this time,' the Laussat's oldest family retainer said, shaking her head and rocking vigorously in her chair. 'Ah remember when he was knee-high to a grasshopper. Had the light of the Devil in his eyes even then.'

Eden sat on her bed hugging herself. She'd never known anyone who had died. Even her grandparents were still alive and indecently healthy. Now Beau Clay was dead: someone she had known, seen, talked about. She shivered. She had been talking about him only last evening. Talking about him when perhaps even then his car had been careering down a darkened, swamp-flanked road.

Her elder sister Romaine came into the room, her face flushed.

'Isn't it terrible? They say his neck was broken and that he drowned! Can you imagine it? Drowning in that terrible swamp, unable to move, just waiting ...'

Eden did not have a very high opinion of her twenty-year-old sister. Faced with Romaine's dramatics, some of Eden's old good sense reasserted itself.

'If he did die like that, there's no need to dwell on it,' she said sharply.

Romaine was about to flounce indignantly from the room at being spoken to in such a manner by a mere seventeen-year-old, but Eden checked her. It was obvious that her mother had been talking about the tragedy and perhaps imparting information she would not give to Eden.

'Was he driving alone?' she asked, trying to close her mind to the dreadful images her sister's revelations had conjured up.

Slightly mollified by being in-the-know, Romaine halted at the door.

'Yes. And they say his father is nearly out of his mind. I mean, everyone in New Orleans knows the future Beau had.'

Eden raised a finely shaped brow and lit a forbidden cigarette. Perdition had been the only future she had heard predicted for Beau Clay. Death, apparently, was already lending enchantment.

Her sister was already gushing on like a child of thirteen.

'He was *so* talented. I guess that's why he was so wild. It takes talented people that way. Think of Scott Fitzgerald. And so *sexy*. Mom said it reminded her of when James Dean died. That . . .'

Eden sighed. There were times when she felt that she was the only sensible person in the house, with the exception of her father. She wanted to discuss Beau Clay's death rationally. And with a semblance of respect.

She wondered if Mae had heard the news. Mae's parents were good friends of Sheriff Surtees. If anyone knew the details of Beau's death, the Jefferson family would. Grabbing her car keys, she excused herself from Romaine's irksome company and left the house. On the drive over to Mae's she considered the possibilities.

Perhaps Beau had had someone with him when he died. Perhaps he had quarrelled with his latest girlfriend. Perhaps he had been drunk or on drugs. Perhaps he had even *meant* to kill himself.

With scant regard for other traffic, she raced her Cadillac down Louisiana Avenue and out towards St George Avenue.

Mae looked distinctly strained. Her usually rosy cheeks were pale, her eyes blue-rimmed.

'We can't talk here,' she whispered to Eden. 'My mother won't leave me alone. She keeps talking and talking about it.'

'Let's go down to Ruby Red's,' Eden said practically. 'We can have hamburgers there and talk undisturbed.'

Mae nodded assent. She, too, wanted to talk about what had happened. She fought back a sudden rush of tears. She'd had a crush on Beau for as long as she could remember, though it had been a secret she had kept to herself. And she had never been obsessed with him as Gussie had.

She froze. 'Gussie!' she said, horrorstruck. 'What about Gussie?'

'I tried to call her but that stupid maid of theirs said she wasn't taking calls.'

'Then she knows?'

'She must do. Her father is a friend of Judge Clay's.'

'You go on down to Ruby Red's,' Eden said decisively. 'That's where all the news will be. I'll go to Gussie. She'll have taken Beau's death badly, especially after last night.'

'Yes.' Mae looked ghastly. 'About last night, Eden. You don't think . . .'

45

'You must come round more often, Eden,' Mrs Jefferson was saying. 'We don't see enough of you. Oh, my, is that the phone again? Please excuse me, girls.'

'Ruby Red's in half an hour,' Eden said, leaving an auguished Mae with tears in her eyes.

'Eden . . .'

The Cadillac door slammed and the engine revved. Mae ran after her but was too late. She halted miserably. She had wanted a quick word with Eden before her courage failed. It would be too late for what she had to say when they were joined by Gussie.

Miserably she reversed her own car out of the Jefferson garage and drove down past City Park and on to their favourite bar on the edge of the French Quarter. It was decorated in the manner of a 1920 speakeasy and though only early, was already crowded, the air full of one topic and one topic alone. Beauregard Clay's untimely death.

Eden motored at her usual high speed back to the Garden District and the Lafayette house that stood way back from the road, screened by palm trees, oaks and lush magnolias.

'Ahm sorry, Miss Eden, but Miss Gussie told me quite particular . . .'

Eden didn't wait for the little maid to finish. At least in the Lafayette household there was no Mrs Lafayette to contend with and Gussie's father would be in his high office block negotiating another deal to enhance the Lafayette bank balance. Impatiently she strode past the protesting girl and headed up the wide staircase towards Gussie's bedroom.

'It's Eden,' she said through the door. 'Can I come in?'

There was no reply. Eden tried the door. It was locked. She swore beneath her breath.

'Please open the door, Gussie. I want to talk to you.'

'I don't want to talk to anyone: not ever again,' a muffled voice said, thick with tears.

Eden leaned against the door and momentarily closed her eyes. 'I thought he was wonderful too, Gussie. I know how you must be feeling. Mae is waiting for us down at Ruby Red's. We can eat there and talk. It will make it easier. You'll be able to pick up a paper, too. There was nothing in this morning's *Figaro*. I guess the news came too late for their first edition, but the *States Item* will have the full story. Come on, Gussie. Please open the door.'

There was a wait that seemed interminable to Eden. Then, very slowly, the key turned in the lock. It was left to Eden to open the door. When she did so her eyes widened, and she stopped. Gussie was wearing the rose-pink gown of the previous evening. Her hair still streamed down past her waist, but this time in wild disarray and not glossy sleekness. She stared at Eden with lifeless eyes.

'He's dead,' she whispered piteously. 'Dead.' Two large tears slid down her face and then Eden circled her in her arms and the dam broke. The tears that shock had refused to release poured down Gussie's face as she sobbed and sobbed.

'How could he die, Eden? How could he die when I love him so much? I shall die, too. I know I shall!' Her voice rose hysterically.

Eden shook her hard. 'Stop talking like that, Augusta Lafayette! He's dead and I don't blame you for crying, but it's not as if it's your father or your boyfriend!'

Gussie wrenched herself away from Eden's grasp, her eyes wild. 'How . . . dare . . . you say such things to me!' she said, gasping the words between her racking sobs. 'He *was* my boyfriend. He was *more* than my boyfriend. He was . . .' She was choking on her own breath.

'He was a man you spoke to only half a dozen times in your life. A man you danced with once. A man who barely knew who you were,' Eden said cruelly.

47

Gussie grasped a bedpost for support. 'He would have loved me! He would! I shall never be able to love anybody else! I shall stay true to him! I shall never forget him! Never!'

'You will,' Eden said with a maturity beyond her years. 'It may seem like the end of the world now but in six months' time you'll barely remember the name of Beau Clay.'

'I will!' Gussie cried vehemently. 'I swear I will!'

'Come on,' Eden said gently. 'Mae is waiting. Change your clothes and come for a drink and something to eat.'

Gussie's tears flowed with fresh impetus. 'How can you talk of eating when Beau is dead? Can't you understand what has happened? Can't you understand that I'll never *see* him again? Never hear his voice?'

'You're overreacting, Gussie. Even if he'd lived, you would only have seen him at a distance or perhaps once a year at your cousin's.'

Gussie threw herself full-length on her bed and beat the pillows with clenched fists.

'I wouldn't! He would have loved me! Oh, Beau! Beau! I wish I were dead too!'

Eden regarded her despairingly. She had known Gussie would react badly to Beau Clay's death, but had not anticipated distress on such a scale. It was patently obvious that she could not take her for a drink and a hamburger when she was in such a state of emotional hysteria. She was weeping unrestrainedly, seemingly oblivious of Eden's presence. Reluctantly Eden left the room and closed the door behind her. For once in her life she felt unable to deal with the situation with which she was confronted.

With none of her usual zest she drove sedately to Esplanade Avenue and squeezed into the crowded bar. More newspapers were out, the headlines screaming Beau's name.

As she made her way through the mass of bodies she heard the same words repeated on every side.

'A tragedy . . .'

'Such a waste . . .'

'Dead, at twenty-seven . . .'

'. . . speed must have been suicidal . . .'

She sat beside Mae and sipped the glass of wine that was pushed across to her.

'Where's Gussie?'

Eden nursed the wine glass. 'Face-down on her bed and crying as if her heart is broken.'

'It probably is,' Mae said compassionately. 'She was head-over-heels in love with him.'

'She barely knew him,' Eden repeated. 'None of us did. He was a film-star figure. Someone whose picture was always in the paper. Someone whose private life was led publicly. You may as well say the women who swooned when Valentino died were in love with *him*. They weren't. They were in love with the *idea* of being in love with him.'

A hint of colour returned to Mae's cheeks.

'I'm glad you said that, Eden. It makes me feel better. I was getting so worried; thinking all kinds of stupid things. Of course Gussie will get over it in time. It's a bit of a shock, that's all.' She managed a tremulous smile and looked towards the door.

'The Shreve boys have just come in. They look dreadful. Were they close to Beau?'

'Not that I know of,' Eden replied drily. 'But I imagine they modelled themselves on him.'

'There's Bradley. He's the only person I've seen so far who doesn't look to be in shock.'

A smile tinged Eden's mouth. It would take a lot to shock Bradley Hampton.

He had seen them and was approaching their table. Mae

shrank back and tried to make herself invisible. Their date had been a disaster. His only interest had been in talking about Gussie.

'Isn't it dreadful?' Eden said as he crossed to their table. 'Have you heard some of the rumours?'

Bradley wasn't remotely interested in rumours.

'Where's Gussie?' he asked with apparent indifference.

Despite herself, Eden felt her nerves begin to throb. There was something overpoweringly masculine about Bradley Hampton. If it wasn't for the fact that she was in love with Dean . . .

'At home, grief-stricken at Beau Clay's death,' Mae said timidly, near to tears. 'It's my belief she'll waste away and die, just like that Frenchwoman in the book we had to read for English Lit.'

Bradley stared down at Eden grim-faced. 'Is that true?'

Eden forced a laugh.

'No. She's a little upset, that's all. She knew Beau slightly. He was a close friend of her cousin Tina's at one time.'

Bradley swung his jacket negligently over one shoulder. He knew just what kind of a friend Beau Clay had been to the provocative Tina Lafayette. He wondered if Gussie did, and doubted it. He took a sip of his beer, turned as his name was called and drifted away.

'He really does care about Gussie, doesn't he?' Mae said enviously. 'I don't understand why she won't date him. He's so handsome, and so . . .' She struggled inadequately for the right word.

'Male,' Eden said obligingly. Bradley Hampton's charms were not lost on her either. 'Restrain your thoughts, Mae. Here comes Austin.'

'What are you girls drinking? White wine?' Austin asked, blinking at them through his thick glasses. 'Let me get

50

another bottle. Nice to see you, Eden. Where have you been lately?'

Eden smiled. 'Around,' she said, wondering when Austin would ask Mae to marry him and when Mae would accept.

'Have you seen the headlines in the paper?' Mae asked as he sat down. 'Do you think he was drunk, Austin? He must have been, mustn't he? I mean, he could drive a car like no one else I've ever seen. How *could* it have happened? He must have been near out of his mind not to have seen a tree that size.'

Eden flicked open a packet of cigarettes and resigned herself to the fact that she was going to hear a lot of talk about the way Beau Clay had met his death. She looked at her wristwatch. It had been three hours since she had left the Lafayette home. Perhaps Gussie would be grateful if she called round now. Excusing herself and leaving Mae in Austin's company, she left the bar.

When she turned into the Lafayette driveway she halted and whistled expressively. Bradley Hampton's distinctive blue Thunderbird was parked conspicuously in front of the porticoed entrance.

So ... Mae was right. Bradley Hampton really *did* care about Gussie. And, on hearing of Gussie's distress, he had driven straight over. It showed a brand of courage Eden admired. She put the Cadillac into reverse and backed out into the Avenue. It seemed as if Gussie was getting all the comfort she needed.

'I wish you'd go away,' Augusta said, her eyes blue hollows in a fragilely pale face. 'I want to be left alone.'

She was sitting on the porch swing. The rose-pink dress had been discarded. Her father would be home soon. Dying of love though she was, she could not allow her father to know. It would cause too many questions, be an invasion of

51

her grief. Instead of her habitual jeans and T-shirt, she wore a white silk dress with a slim, gold rouleau belt. Her hair had been carelessly caught in a ribbon in the nape of her neck. Her face was devoid of make-up. Bradley thought she had never looked so beautiful.

'I thought you might like dinner tonight; at Agostino's.'

A flicker of interest pierced Gussie's grief. She wondered how Bradley Hampton knew she had a penchant for Sicilian food. She'd cried for so long that she couldn't remember when last she'd eaten. Agostino's did a marvellous *Spiedini Al serri-Rotoli*. For a moment she was tempted and then she remembered Beau and that he was dead and that she was going to devote the rest of her life to grief.

Tears hovered in her violet-dark eyes. 'If you don't leave I'll call Louis and have him remove you.'

A brief smile touched Bradley's mouth. 'I think he would find that a little difficult, Gussie. I don't leave anywhere unless it's of my own free will.'

Gussie blinked back her tears and looked across at him. She had never realized before how tall he was, or how broad-shouldered. Nearly as broad-shouldered as Beau.

'You've overstayed your welcome, Bradley Hampton,' she said, springing to her feet, her eyes filling with tears. 'I don't want you to come here again. I don't want anyone to come and see me. Not ever again.' Covering her face with her hands, she rushed into the house and the sound of her sobs could be heard fading into the distance until at last her bedroom door silenced them.

Bradley remained on the porch, a savagery on his usually good-humoured features that would have stunned his friends and shocked even Gussie. Damn Beau Clay. He was exercising as powerful an effect on Gussie dead as he had when he had been alive. His eyes blazed with fierce determination. He would take no notice of Gussie's request.

He would come back tomorrow and the next day and the next. He would come back until she had forgotten her dream of Beau Clay, and until she fell in love with flesh and blood reality: until she fell in love with him.

In her room, above her sobs, Gussie heard his car door slam and the engine rev. She ran to the window and peeped surreptitiously outside. It was strange that she had never noticed before how handsome Bradley Hampton was. But not as handsome as Beau. No one was as handsome as Beau had been.

She sank onto the bed and began to sob bitterly, remembering Beau's devastating down-slanting smile, the way he had held her at the New Year party, the feel of his body close to hers.

At her request, the maid told her father that she had a headache and did not want to be disturbed. As the evening drew on into night she gave herself up to grief for Beau Clay, but occasionally, insidiously, his lean dark face merged with that of Bradley Hampton's. Angry whenever it did so, she buried her face in her pillows, reminding herself that she was inconsolable. That the rest of her life was to be spent in grief for Beau.

CHAPTER THREE

Beauregard Clay was buried by his grieving father and a multitude of friends three days later. In death he had taken on a stature that he had never enjoyed in life. His father would have liked the ceremony to have a semblance of privacy but that proved to be impossible. The staid and respectable felt it their duty to be present, and Beau's contemporaries came from as far away as La Jolla and New York. Not until they actually saw the lifeless body being laid to rest in the family mausoleum would they be able to believe that Beau was really dead. Young women the Judge had never set eyes on before wept uncontrollably as the cortège made its way to the St Louis Cemetery in Basin Street, where the Clay mausoleum had stood, receiving its family members, since the city had been founded on the swamp beneath its streets. Judge Clay had no intention of burying his wayward son elsewhere.

The Judge's face was haggard, deep lines etched from nose to mouth and furrowing his brow as his elder, remaining son, walked at his side. The storm clouds that could blow up with such unexpectedness and ferocity over the city, threatened in the distance.

When the cortège reached the cemetery Beau's out-of-state friends eyed their surroundings uneasily. The usual swift, neat cremations amongst rose-laid gardens had been no preparation for Beau's burial. Monolithic tombs, like tenements, towered above the ground. The dead seemed literally to press in on them on either side and more than one New Yorker wished he hadn't made the trip.

Mae Jefferson stood beside her mother, shivering despite the steaming heat of the afternoon. She had not wanted to come but her mother had been adamant. Respect had to be shown. Besides, the Judge would notice which families had attended and which had not, and he was a very influential man.

Mae looked away as the priest officiated beside the ebony casket lying on the catafalque, not listening as the well-known words rolled sonorously over the bowed heads around her. In the distance she could see the tomb of Etienne de Bore, the first planter to make sugar a commercial enterprise in the South. And somewhere, unknown and unmarked, lay the rotting bones of Marie Laveau, infamous Voodoo Queen of Old New Orleans.

Her grandmother had told her many tales of Marie Laveau and her supernatural powers: tales her mother discounted and refused to listen to. But Mae knew voodoo was real. Her grandmother had told her so.

There was a distant rumble of thunder and a few of the bowed heads turned, eyeing the sky and calculating how long it would be before they were caught in a torrential downpour. Tina Lafayette's sobs were heard above the noise. Charles Lafayette stood apart from her, disassociating himself from a spectacle that could only give rise to gossip. There was no sign of Gussie.

Mae closed her eyes and dug her nails into her palms. She hated her mother for forcing her to endure such an ordeal. Somewhere in the vast crowd she had seen Eden's dark head and wished that Eden were standing next to her.

'. . . ashes to ashes, dust to dust . . .'

The macabre, swathed corpse was ceremoniously lifted from the coffin and carried into the giant mausoleum. There it was placed on a stone shelf. The hot, dry air would accomplish the rest.

The sun-tanned blonde from La Jolla screamed and was hastily shushed by those around her. New Orleans burials were unlike any other. There was no room, no suitable burying land, for the luxury of coffins.

The mausoleum was sealed, the iron gates swung into place. Judge Clay looked momentarily disorientated and then walked with pathetic dignity back through the overgrown churchyard and towards his limousine, the mourners parting silently as they made way for him.

In the Lafayette mansion Gussie lay prostrate on the bed she had barely left since hearing of Beau's death. Gold velvet drapes were drawn across the window, plunging the room into dark shadow. In her imagination she followed the funeral procession every step of the way, from the elegant Clay home to Beau's final resting place amongst his ancestors. She knew that Eden was going with her mother; that Mae was going with hers. She knew that her father, out of respect for Judge Clay, was also attending. She, too, could have been there, but she could not have borne to be only one of a nameless crowd. To have her tears regarded on the same level as Mae's. She wanted to wear a black dress and black silk stockings and a heavy veil over her face. She wanted people to be in awe of her grief: to feel their compassion for her suffering. To realize that she was the only person Beau Clay would have ever loved. She wanted to place a single rose on the lifeless body, to cry in private beside him.

She could not do so and so she did not go. She wept alone, convinced that joy would never enter her heart again.

'I'm taking Gussie to Al Hirt's Club on Bourbon Street later this evening, sir,' Bradley said with the casual confidence that was an integral part of his personality. 'The show doesn't start till ten-thirty so it will be pretty late before I bring her home. I just wanted you to know I'll take good care of her.'

'I see.' Charles Lafayette regarded Bradley Hampton over the broad expanse of his desk in the book-lined study. The jazz haunts of the city held no charm for him. He preferred the New Orleans Symphony Orchestra but despite taking Gussie several times, he had not been able to impart his love of classical music to his daughter. Normally, he would not have countenanced her going out to a jazz club until the early hours. However, Bradley Hampton wasn't just any young man. He was an extremely personable one, and if he could lift Gussie from the strange depression from which she had been suffering this last month, Charles would be more than grateful to him.

Gussie's father rose from behind his desk and held out his hand to Bradley. 'Just make sure you keep your word, my boy.'

Bradley clasped the hand firmly and grinned. Charles Lafayette would have his hide if he didn't keep his word. Besides, when it came to sex, it could be had easily and often any time of the day or night. He wanted something a little more from Gussie. Just what, he wasn't yet prepared to admit, even to himself. Early marriage had never been part of his schemes for the future. But then neither had Gussie.

'How dare you speak to my father behind my back!' Gussie hissed. 'I wouldn't go to Al Hirt's with you if you were the last man on earth!'

'I'll pick you up at nine o'clock,' Bradley said calmly.

Gussie stamped a foot. 'Are you deaf, Bradley Hampton? I said I wouldn't . . .'

He covered the distance between them in one stride and grasped her wrist so hard that she cried out in pain.

'I heard you, Gussie,' he said, and something hot flickered at the back of his eyes. 'Be ready when I come, and put some lipstick on. I like my girls to look special, not like colourless rabbits.'

Gussie gasped and fell back against the wall. He grinned, letting go of her, and strode, whistling, from the house.

Colourless rabbit! How *dare* he? Trembling with rage, Gussie stalked to her bedroom and sat in front of her dressing-table mirror. Her hair no longer shimmered so that it was the envy of all her friends. It had begun to look lifeless, hanging unbrushed and uncared for. Her eyes, with their thick sweep of dark lashes, were blue-shadowed, her cheeks pale. She looked as plain as Mae. Furiously, she picked up her silver-backed hairbrush and began to brush her hair vigorously. She was Augusta Lafayette. The acknowledged belle of her friends. At Mardi Gras she had been Queen of the Carnival: and Bradley Hampton had the nerve to indicate he was doing her a favour by escorting her in public!

When Bradley arrived at the Lafayette home at nine o'clock that evening, Charles Lafayette had a companionable glass of bourbon with him and was suitably pleased when his daughter finally put in an appearance at nine-thirty.

She was wearing a deceptively simple dress with a cowl neckline that brought discreet attention to the perfection of her breasts. The skirt fell softly over her hips; she was stockingless, her sun-tanned legs gleaming, her toenails lacquered a pearly pink. Her hair hung silkily down her back, her lips glossed, her lashes mascara-ed. She smiled sweetly at her father and glared malevolently at Bradley. But Bradley was indifferent, and, bidding Gussie's father good-night, ushered her into his Thunderbird, not even bothering to remark on her appearance.

Gussie seethed and vowed to hold on to her anger. She did, but it had no effect. Bradley was obviously intent on having a good time, whether she was or not. There were friends of his at the club that she had never seen before. Friends far more sophisticated than she had anticipated. There were women too. Beautiful and sleek, and there was no mistaking the reaction when their eyes rested on Bradley's dark good looks. It was nice to be the object of so much female envy.

Despite herself, Gussie began to enjoy the evening.

By the time it was 3 a.m. and Bradley was saying goodbye to the friends they had joined, Gussie was reluctant to leave. Bradley merely shrugged and propelled her out into the sultry night air. By the time he got Gussie home and indoors, it would be four. He didn't want to push his luck with Charles Lafayette too far.

'That music was just great,' she said dreamily as they sped down Bourbon Street and out of the French Quarter. 'Do you go there often?'

'Enough.'

She slid her eyes across at him in the dark. There was a negligence about Bradley that was intensely arousing. He had made no effort to attract the attention of the girls who had flocked around him. He was making no effort with her now. He was not heading out to the darkened lakeside as any other escort would have done. She had a strange feeling that he was not even going to attempt to kiss her goodnight. Looking at his mouth as the car flashed beneath the streetlights, she felt a surge of disappointment. There was no hint of cruelty about it, as there had been about Beau's. No hardness. Bradley smiled easily and often and yet the sensuality was undeniable. She wondered what it would be like to kiss him, and then clenched her hands tightly in her lap. How *could* she think such things with Beau only dead a month? Hadn't she vowed to grieve for him until the day she died? The Thunderbird turned into the oak-lined driveway of her home and she suppressed a sigh. Secretly,

59

though she wouldn't admit it to anyone but herself, there were moments that she forgot Beau. Tonight she hadn't thought of him for hours. Until now.

Bradley turned to her as he halted the car. Gussie stiffened. Now she would have the pleasure of proving her fidelity.

'Goodnight, Gussie,' Bradley said, a hint of laughter in his voice as he walked round and opened her car door for her. 'Thanks for a nice evening.'

Gussie was nonplussed. That had been *her* line, delivered archly and coldly, rocketing him to disappointment because he had been cheated of a goodnight kiss. Feeling slightly foolish she stepped on to the gravel.

'Be seeing you,' he said, and as she walked up the steps to the bronze-hinged mahogany door, he waved casually, got back into his car and sped away as if he had been depositing a parcel.

Gussie's cheeks flamed with angry colour. He hadn't even *attempted* to kiss her. He hadn't even held her hand. What kind of boy was he? She flounced up to her room and savagely began lathering her face with cleansing cream. He wasn't a boy. He was a man. That much was clear by the way every female eye had been drawn to him at the jazz club. Then why hadn't he driven her to the darkened lake shore? Why hadn't he attempted to make love to her? Why hadn't he kissed her goodnight? Gussie climbed into bed and stared at the ceiling. He had kissed Mae. Mae had told her so. Mae had *said* that nothing further had happened, but there was no way Gussie could be completely sure. Why should Bradley want to kiss Mae and not want to kiss her? It didn't make sense. For the first time in a month she went to sleep with her mind full of someone other than Beau.

It was two weeks before Bradley got in touch with Gussie again, two weeks in which she had begun to suffer from headaches and to feel uneasy for no reason. Often, when walking with Mae or Eden, she would suddenly swing her head round as if someone had called her name. No one ever had, and Eden and Mae would exchange silent glances. But when Bradley finally called, Gussie suddenly felt free of that nameless anxiety that so constantly beset her. Bradley wanted only to take her out for an hour, to Audubon Park. It was nowhere special – had it been anyone else she would have felt insulted – but that afternoon she enjoyed herself. They wandered beside the winding lagoons and sat on the edge of one of the fountains, enjoying the fine spray that showered their heads and shoulders. They picnicked, surrounded by flowers and with a magnificent view of the Mississippi curving lazily seaward, and the hour stretched to two and then to three. They went into the zoo and fed nuts to the monkeys and watched the graceful prowling of the Bengal tiger. When Bradley led the way back to the car she felt flooded with disappointment.

The car doors clicked shut. Bradley adjusted his driving mirror. His shirt was open at the neck and she could see the strong muscles of his chest. She had an overwhelming urge to reach out and touch his skin. Feel the warmth of his flesh next to hers. She wondered why she had so consistently refused to date him and could not quite remember. 'I'm meeting the Shreves and Austin and Mae at Ruby Red's this evening,' Bradley said, turning to look at her. 'Do you fancy coming?'

'Oh yes! I'd love to!' Her eagerness had been spontaneous and unthinking. She flushed.

His white teeth flashed in a smile. 'I'll pick you up at seven.'

'Yes. Thank you.' She struggled to sound off-hand and fumbled for a cigarette.

He flicked his lighter and leaned across, steadying her

hand. Their eyes met. At his touch she had started to tremble. Seeing his look of intense desire, the blood burned in her veins.

'I love you, Augusta Lafayette,' he said softly, oblivious of the families piling in and out of the cars parked around them. 'I love you and some day I'm going to marry you.' And then he switched the car into life, sweeping out into St Charles Avenue and towards the Lafayette home before Gussie could even catch her breath.

The Shreve boys made her laugh. Mae, whose hand barely left Austin's for the whole of the evening, was overjoyed to see her. It was good to be out again; to be the centre of attention; to know that if she wanted, she could have both Don and Jason Shreve eating out of the palm of her hand. Her spine tingled with suppressed excitement. It was good to be with Bradley, too. She wondered if he'd meant what he'd said to her that afternoon. There was nothing in his manner now to indicate that he had. Desirée Ashington, the local siren, had made a bee-line for him the minute they had entered, greeting him with undue familiarity. He had not seemed to object. Even now he seemed to be enjoying her attention. Her halter top was indecently low. Gussie pretended not to notice the intimacy of their conversation but Mae's eyes were sympathetic. Desirée had even tried to add Austin's scalp to her collection. She had failed and it had been then that Mae had agreed to marry him. At last Mae knew he wasn't just going out with her until someone prettier came along. He loved her, just as he said he did.

Desirée continued to dominate Bradley's attention and the angrier Gussie became, the more she hid it, laughing with apparent delight at an inane joke of Austin's, raising the Shreve boys' hopes by giving them her undivided attention.

As Bradley drove her home she sank into outraged silence, her shoulders tense, her hands clasped tightly around her knees. Instead of taking the turning for her home, Bradley continued to drive out of the city and towards the woods and the lakeside. It was what Gussie had secretly wanted him to do ever since their first date. She swung round in her seat.

'Just where do you think you are going, Bradley Hampton?'

Bradley changed gear, slipped a look into his driving mirror and said leisurely, 'Taking you somewhere quiet and dark so I can kiss the hell out of you.'

Gussie choked, her eyes glazing. 'You turn this car round immediately, Bradley Hampton! If you want to take anyone to the woods, take Desirée! She'd love every minute of it!'

'I dare say she would,' Bradley agreed with infuriating calm. 'Only I'm not taking Desirée, I'm taking you.'

'Oh no you're not! I'm not one of your cheap little tarts! One of your easy pick-ups!'

The city lights were behind them. The road was shadowed by trees and was dark. Bradley pulled over to the verge and switched off the engine.

'I never made a habit of going out with tarts,' he said, his lazy Southern drawl suddenly very pronounced. 'Neither have I ever made it a habit to go out with people who bore me. I'm very likely to do just as you demand, Gussie, and turn the car around and drive you home. Because that's what you're beginning to do – bore me.'

Gussie sobbed and drew back her hand to deliver a stinging blow to his cheek. Her wrist was caught in a steel-like grip. There was amusement in his blue eyes.

'If I didn't know you better, Augusta Lafayette, I'd say you were jealous.'

Gussie struggled but could not free herself. 'How dare you say such a thing! Me? Jealous of Desirée? And because of you?' The more she writhed to escape his grip, the more his amusement deepened.

'I think I've been patient with you long enough, Gussie.' His eyes lingered on her mouth and a little pulse began to beat wildly in her throat. At last he was going to kiss her. Against her will and by force.

'I meant what I said this afternoon, Gussie, and before I take you home this evening, you're going to say the same thing to me.'

'No . . .' Her breath was coming in harsh gasps. 'Never!'

She tried to pull away from him, but he held her easily, his mouth coming down on hers in swift, unfumbled contact. She twisted violently, freeing one arm, but instead of pushing him away she circled his neck, her lips parting willingly beneath his, her body aflame with the desire that had previously existed only in her imagination.

'Gussie, sweet, darling Gussie.'

There was a depth of feeling in his voice that startled her. This was no casual encounter. This was the real thing. This was Bradley Hampton telling her he loved her. That he wanted to marry her. Bradley Hampton who was heir to millions; whose family was as prestigious as the Lafayettes. Bradley Hampton, whom every girl in New Orleans would have given a year of her life to date. Bradley Hampton, who had dark hair and laughing blue eyes, and whom her father would approve of.

He wound his fingers in her hair, pulling her head back so she was forced to meet his compelling gaze.

'Tell me you love me, Gussie.'

There was a menacing edge to his voice.

Gussie wanted him to kiss her again, to feel the sweetness of his lips on hers.

His hand twisted tightly in her hair. *'Tell me, Gussie!'*

Desperately she thought of Beau, but Beau was dead. Beau

64

would never hold her as Bradley did. Beau would never kiss her until her bones melted.

'I love you,' she whispered helplessly. 'I love you, and I'll marry you.'

The Hamptons were pleased. Mrs Hampton had not anticipated her only son marrying so young, but, she reflected, Bradley had never yet made a decision he had regretted. Mr Hampton silently congratulated himself for his good fortune. Augusta Lafayette was one of the three daughters-in-law to whom he had secretly given his seal of approval.

Charles Lafayette, after a few days' speculation, was also pleased. Gussie had begun to worry him lately. She had continued to be unusually withdrawn and introspective. Brooding when she should have been laughing. Silent when she should have been gaily chattering. Marriage to Bradley Hampton would dispel her moroseness. There was a likeable maturity about Bradley. He would make Gussie happy. And there would be no more sleepless nights worrying about fortune hunters and other such undesirables.

Mae was slightly disappointed that Gussie had not done as she had promised, and devoted her life to unrequited love. It would have been so romantic. She used to sink into unusual silence whenever anyone mentioned Beau Clay's name, but, fortunately, her fears had proved groundless. She was glad she had not divulged them to the practical Eden. Gussie was blatantly happy. Bradley would look after her.

Gussie was in seventh heaven. First there was her eighteenth birthday party in August and then there was her wedding to look forward to. It was planned for October and was eagerly entered into social diaries.

All through the hot, sultry summer, Gussie told her friends that she had never been so happy in her life. At the masqued balls and parties, the parades and barbecues, she was like a diamond, a host of facets seeming to sparkle at once as she laughed and danced, her handsome husband-to-be at her side.

'Everything is perfect, just perfect,' she said happily to Mae and Eden as she swung on the old porch swing. 'I never dreamed I could be so happy.'

'I'm going to marry Austin early next year,' Mae said, sipping on her iced mint julep. She giggled. 'Mrs Mae Merriweather. It's quite a mouthful isn't it? What's the matter, Gussie? You're not listening to me.'

Gussie had halted the gentle rocking of the swing and was looking around her with a bewildered expression in her eyes.

It's nothing Mae. I just thought someone called my name.'

'For goodness' sake. I thought you'd stopped all that ages ago. Look at your arms. You've got goose bumps. There must be something wrong with your blood.'

A dragon-fly hovered above them in the motionless air.

Gussie rubbed her arms and sat down, her eyes troubled. 'I keep thinking someone's *looking* at me. It's most weird.'

'Someone usually is,' Eden said complacently, swirling the ice cubes round in her glass. 'With your hair and eyes you can't expect anything else.'

Gussie laughed, dismissing the uneasy feeling that assailed her with such unpleasant regularity.

'Let's have another drink. We're big girls now,' Eden said, wondering if she should point out to Gussie that Bradley was uncannily like Beau in lots of respects. Not as intimidating, of course. There was nothing satanic in Bradley's handsomeness. Still, he had a way of commanding respect from even the oldest and most revered of New Orleans citizens, and his thick black hair and teasing eyes were nearly as devastating as Beau's film-star looks had been. But Eden kept her thoughts to herself. She alone had seen the extent of Gussie's hysteria after Beau Clay's death. It would be a long time before she forgot the sight of Gussie, her eyes vacant with grief, her hair tumbling around her shoulders in wild disarray, her gown the one she had worn for the silly ritual the night before. Even to think of it caused the nape of her neck to prickle unpleasantly.

'Only the best French champagne,' Charles Lafayette said sternly over the phone to the caterers. 'I don't want any corner-cutting.'

He rose from his desk, puffing on a cigar as he strode to the study windows that overlooked St Michel's rolling lawns. He'd planned everything himself, down to the last detail. Gussie's birthday party was going to be the most memorable event of the year – apart from her wedding. There were going to be no hired, second-rate musicians playing at *his* daughter's big day. He'd paid for the best there was, and it had cost him. He didn't care. He puffed on his cigar contentedly. He'd gone as far as Houston for the experts who were mounting the firework display. Gussie had gone to Paris with his sister Tina for her dress. He smiled a rare smile. Tina had spent even more than Gussie on their whirlwind trip across the Atlantic. Invitations to the party had been practically begged for by the most elite of New Orleans. The guest list had been ruthless, composed almost entirely of families whose names went back to the days of the Battle of New Orleans. Gallatins and St Clairs; Lafittes and Delatours. Far-flung Lafayettes were going to meet together for the first time in living memory. Cousins and second-cousins, uncles and great-uncles, aunts and nieces had been summoned from every corner of the globe, their travelling expenses paid for by himself, and all had eagerly accepted.

It was going to be a party to end all parties and Augusta was going to look magnificent. He rocked back on his heels in satisfaction. His little girl. She'd looked like a fairy princess at Mardi Gras. She would look like a dream come true on the night of her birthday. Cigar smoke wreathed his head. Nothing had ever blighted Augusta's life. Nothing ever would. He wouldn't allow it. Not as long as he had breath in his body.

He turned once more and sat at his desk. The flower arrangements for the house and garden still had to be decided upon. For dramatic effect he had stipulated that every bloom must be white. It would be a stunning contrast to the more usual riots of colour.

'I had to practically plead with Daddy to allow Eden and her parents to come to my birthday party,' Gussie said happily, her arm wound through Bradley's as they strolled through City Park. She giggled. 'He actually referred to them as upstart Yankees, and they're French Canadians. Can you imagine how mad Mr Alexander would be if he knew? Daddy also allowed invitations to go to the Jeffersons, although he wasn't happy about it. Mrs Jefferson isn't his favourite person, but he was very nice about it, considering . . .'

'Considering what?' Bradley asked, gazing down at her with amusement.

The smile faded from Gussie's face and a troubled expression touched her eyes. 'Oh, he's never liked the fact that Mae is my closest friend.'

Bradley raised a querying brow. 'Why? The Jeffersons are pillars of New Orleans society and have been from time immemorial.'

'I know. It's silly.' Her arm tightened around his waist. 'It's just that years ago Mae's grandmother and mine were as close as sisters and . . .'

68

'And what?' Bradley asked tenderly.

She gave a little shrug. 'Mae's grandmother went dotty and lives all alone, way out in the bayous and my grandmother . . .'

Bradley waited expectantly.

Gussie forced a smile. 'My grandmother died young.'

Committed suicide: drowned herself. Should she tell him? Would he think her grandmother as crazy as Mae's?

To tell him now would spoil their sun-filled afternoon. She would tell him later. Bradley wouldn't mind. He loved her too much to mind about a thing like that.

The shadow touched her lightly, the whisper barely audible. She swung round swiftly.

'Hey, what is it?' Bradley asked, steadying her. 'You'll twist an ankle doing that.'

'Did you see it, Bradley?' she asked urgently, all thoughts of her grandmother vanishing, her face strained. 'It's gone now, but it was there, I swear it was!'

Bradley frowned, circling her shoulders with his arms and feeling her tremble. 'What was, sweetheart?'

Gussie shivered. 'A shadow. It falls across me from nowhere. You must have seen it.'

He shook his head, pulling gently at her arm, but she remained standing in the pathway, gazing round her with bewildered eyes. 'It's always happening, Bradley. It makes me feel so strange. There's never anybody there.'

Bradley shrugged. 'Then there's nothing to worry about,' he said reasonably.

'Yes, but . . .' She halted. She couldn't tell Bradley that she kept hearing her name called. Her eyes swept the pathway and gardens once more. There was no one within two hundred yards of them. Reluctantly she turned and continued walking.

'But what?' Bradley prompted.

'Nothing,' Gussie said miserably. 'I guess it was my imagination after all.'

Bradley gave her a searching look. It wasn't the first time Gussie had swung round to face someone who was not there. Her nerves were getting jumpy and he blamed her father. He was making far too much of an event of her birthday party. He pulled her head down on his shoulder. When they were married there would be no repeat of the Paris nonsense. If Gussie went away it would be with him. Charles Lafayette might love her to idolatry, but Charles didn't know what was best for her. He, Bradley, did. The scent of her hair sent the blood coursing through his veins. He was going to love her and look after her for the rest of his life.

'Eighteen years old,' Charles Lafayette said his eyes suspiciously bright as he gave her a birthday kiss. 'I find it hard to believe, Augusta. It seems only yesterday that you were a baby.'

A spasm of pain crossed his face as he thought of his long-dead wife and the pleasure she would have gained from their beautiful daughter if she had lived.

'This was your mother's,' he said gently, handing her a satin-ribboned box. 'I bought if for her on our first wedding anniversary.'

'Oh Daddy!' Gussie's violet-dark eyes glowed. Reverently she undid the satin bow and lifted the white embossed lid.

The bracelet lay on a bed of black velvet, diamonds and sapphires flashing as if with an inner life.

Gussie gasped and lifted the bracelet from the box. She allowed her father to clasp it around her wrist. In link after link, diamonds circled sapphires like petals around the hearts of flowers.

'It's beautiful, Daddy. I've never seen anything so lovely. Not ever.'

Charles Lafayette smiled indulgently. 'It will have to be returned to the bank vault after this evening, I'm afraid. It's much too valuable to be kept in the house.'

'But I can wear it tonight, Daddy, can't I?' Her pretty face was anxious.

He laughed. 'Of course you may, darling. Tonight you're going to be a princess.'

She kissed his cheek and then sat, long after he had left the breakfast room, gazing at the breathtaking stones that encircled her wrist. Her mother, too, must have sat thus, overwhelmed at the beauty that had been given to her. Love welled up in her. Love for the mother she had never known. Love for her father. Love for Bradley. Tonight was going to be wonderful. The most wonderful night of her life.

'Now you sit still so I don't muss up your hair,' Allie chided, slipping the billowing confection of taffeta and tulle over Augusta's head. 'My, my, but this surely is some dress. I reckon even Kreeger's don't get dresses in like this.'

'This dress is a Dior original,' Gussie said, stepping in front of her full-length mirror and turning first one way and then another. 'Isn't is gorgeous, Allie? Have you ever seen anything so divine?'

'I can't say that I have,' Allie said truthfully, surveying the delicately ruched bodice of pale lemon, the shoulder straps so fine that they seemed non-existent.

Gussie twirled around and the layered ballerina skirts of hand embroidered tulle floated ethereally around her like a cloud. Ecstatically she slipped her sheer stockinged feet into a pair of white satin slippers. Her nails were laquered palest pink, her lips glossed prettily. On her wrist the bracelet sparkled and shone. She looked a million dollars and knew it.

Tingling with excitement she gave one last look in the

mirror and walked slowly out onto the landing and towards the head of the curving staircase.

Bradley was at the foot and the expression in his eyes sent a warm flush to her cheeks. Her father and Tina stood beside him and there was a concerted intake of breath from the assembled household staff as she appeared. Horatio, the chauffeur, began to sing 'Happy Birthday' and everyone, her father included, joined in.

Almost shyly she descended the stairs and was given birthday kisses from every member of the staff, from Louis, the butler, to Sabina Royal, the cook.

Orchids and roses and freesias banked the marble hallway, the scent heady in the early evening air. Outside thousands of the same plants had been specially bedded so that St Michel's vast grounds were a symphony of white blossom interspersed with twinkling fairylights.

The breath caught in the back of Bradley's throat as he took her hand. She had never looked more beautiful. Happiness seemed to radiate from her. The glow in her eyes put the jewels on her wrist to shame. Her hair gleamed like spun gold. She was the princess from the fairy stories of his childhood. He wanted to kiss her more than he had wanted anything else in the world but he could not. Her father was watching them benignly. Her guests were waiting.

'I love you,' he whispered to her as they stepped outside and the band began to play. 'I could no more live without you than cease to breathe.'

Her fingers interlocked with his. The heat of his body seemed to flare through her. 'Happy Birthday' was being sung again. She was inundated with presents and good wishes. She laughed and smiled and wished that she were alone with Bradley. Desire had sprung up in her like a flame. She wanted more than kisses and caresses. She wanted to be made love to. She wanted to belong to Bradley body and soul.

'Darling Augusta, you look absolutely wonderful,' Natalie Jefferson gushed, kissing her on both cheeks.

'That dress!' Eden's mother said wonderingly. 'I've never seen anything so exquisite. Did it come from New York?'

'Paris,' Gussie said, removing herself from a warm embrace and moving on to pay her respects to her Lafayette relations as Mrs Alexander watched her with envy in her eyes.

'Paris,' she whispered to her husband. 'Can you imagine it? A Paris gown at eighteen.'

'Very pretty,' her husband agreed, his eyes straying appreciatively over the scores of young girls who flocked around like so many butterflies.

Eden was wearing a searing pink gown of shot silk taffeta, strapless and ruched with such full skirts that it was impossible for her to sit down. Mae was unexpectedly pretty in a pale-blue, demurely high-necked dress that fell in soft folds over her full hips. A Burmese pearl necklace was her only jewellery and Austin escorted her proudly. Mae was evolving her own style of dressing and it was one that suited her. Desirée Ashington had abandoned demureness altogether. Her figure-hugging black dress was split to the navel, revealing a cleavage that left Mr Alexander breathless.

The cream of New Orleans society glided in and out of the lavish marquee, the men elegant in tuxedos, the women alluring in diaphanous pastels.

Family heirlooms had been removed from vaults and safes. Diamonds and rubies vied with amethysts and pearls. Earrings, necklaces, bracelets, brooches, studs and pendants glittered and shone.

The band struck up the first waltz of the evening and Bradley led Gussie away from her doting relatives. He held her closely in his arms, dancing her round and round as the evening sky took on a bluish tinge and the first sprinkling of stars began to gleam. Her breasts rose temptingly from the bodice of her gown.

'Do you know what you do to my temperature dancing next to me half-naked?' Bradley said, tightening his arms around her.

'Sssh,' Gussie giggled. 'Someone will hear you.'

His lips brushed her temples and she closed her eyes blissfully. She was the envy of all her friends. The luckiest girl in New Orleans.

The waltz changed to a quickstep, a foxtrot, a waltz again. Reluctantly Bradley released her and allowed her to dance with a procession of uncles and cousins. Dusk turned to night. Fireflies danced amongst the trees; a galaxy of fairylights illuminated St Michel's lawns as dance followed dance.

With a flourish Charles Lafayette bade the musicians refresh themselves with pink champagne and ordered that the firework display should begin.

There were gasps of delight and screams of pleasure as giant Roman candles whoosed into the air, scattering golden rain; as enormous Catherine wheels spun in galaxies of colour; as rockets trailed crimson streaks across the sky. Then, as everyone laughingly held flaring sparklers, Gussie's birthday cake was brought ceremoniously from the house. Circled by hundreds of relatives and friends Gussie cut the first piece and then, as the last of the fireworks died away, entered Bradley's arms as the band began to play 'Blue Moon'.

'Happy, sweetheart?' he asked tenderly, his lips touching her ivory-pale hair.

'Oh yes!' Her eyes shone as she lifted her face to his.

Her lips were parted. Soft and inviting. Unheeding of the

guests who danced and laughed and chatted around them Bradley lowered his head to hers. Joy surged through her. She loved him so much it was a physical pain. Slowly he lifted his head from hers, his teasing blue eyes dark with need.

'I love you, Gussie. I shall always love you.'

She traced the strong outline of his jaw with her fingertips 'I love you, too, Brad. And I shall forever and forever and for—'

One moment his face was above her and the next it was spiralling into the distance. She was falling amidst a vortex of brilliant colours and black rushing winds. She tried to call his name but no sound would come from her throat. The colours clashed and seared against the back of her eyes. The wind deafened her, sucking her down so that she could hardly breathe. Vainly her hands sought to hold on to him and failed. The colours vanished. Only darkness remained.

'*Gussie!*' He seized hold of her as she fell, scooping her up into his arms, and ran white-faced through the mass of startled dancers and towards the house.

'What happened? Did Gussie faint?'

'I've never seen anything like it. She went out like a light.'

'Is she sick? What if . . .'

The music faltered and, at a frantic signal from Tina Lafayette, continued playing, barely audible above the buzz of speculation.

'Find Dr Meredith,' Charles Lafayette snapped, hurrying after Bradley as he carried an unconscious Gussie into the main drawing room. 'He was down near the pool. Get him here immediately!'

As Bradley laid her on a sofa, Gussie moaned, her lashes fluttering, her carefully manicured hands reaching up to her throat as if it had been bruised.

75

'Water,' Bradley ordered a dazed aunt, without releasing his hold on Gussie or taking his eyes from her face. 'Fetch her some water.'

Charles Lafayette moved forward, attempting to take his daughter from Bradley's grasp. Bradley ignored him as if he were no more than one of the guests. The glass of water was proffered over the shoulders of over a dozen anxious relatives.

'Here, sweetheart. Drink this.' Gently Bradley lifted her head.

The long lashes stirred again and then opened, wide dark eyes staring around in frightened bewilderment.

'I'm here, Gussie.'

Her eyes met his and she sobbed, flinging her arms around his neck, sending the glass of water flying to the floor. 'Oh Brad! Brad! Hold me! Please hold me!'

Charles Lafayette cleared his throat and wished to God there weren't so many witnesses to his daughter's distress.

'What happened, darling?' He was rocking her in his arms with the tenderness of absolute love.

'I don't know. I suddenly felt so cold and sick . . .'

Dr Meredith pushed his way through Lafayettes and Delatours and knelt at the side of the sofa. With strong, capable hands he felt her pulse, took her temperature and then rose to his feet with a sign of relief. From the garbled message he had received, he had expected to find Gussie on the point of death. Already the colour was returning to her cheeks.

'A faint,' he said reassuringly to Charles Lafayette, and then, echoing the words of the elderly cousin, pronounced, 'Too much excitement. There's nothing to worry about.'

Gussie sipped at the water and gazed at him with anxious eyes. 'Can I go back outside, Dr Meredith? I feel all right now. Truly I do.'

Jim Meredith smiled. 'I'd be the last one to spoil your party, Augusta. As soon as you feel the strength return to your legs you can go and continue dancing. But no champagne!'

Gussie managed a tremulous smile. 'I promise.'

A new expression entered her eyes. 'You don't think people will think it was the champagne that caused me to faint, do you? I've had only two glasses and I don't think I finished either of them.'

'They'd better not,' Charles Lafayette said grimly. 'Are you sure she should continue dancing, Jim? Wouldn't it be safer if she went to bed?'

'At my birthday party?' Gussie cried, swinging her legs off the sofa. 'Daddy, you couldn't be so mean!'

Jim Meredith patted Charled Lafayette on the shoulder. 'She's all right, Charles. Believe me. If I thought there was the slightest cause for alarm I'd order her to bed, party or no party.'

Gussie rose determinedly to her feet, supported by Bradley's steadying arm.

'I'm fine, really I am. Just a little wobbly, and that will pass off in a minute. Mae is *always* fainting. I used to think it quite romantic, but I don't any longer. It's hideous.'

'Here's a shawl for you, darling,' Tina Lafayette said, handing her a gossamer-light, delicately fringed wrap.

Gussie laughed. 'No thank you, Cousin Tina. I don't need a shawl yet. I'll save that for my eightieth birthday party, not my eighteenth.' She grasped Bradley's hand. 'Don't look so worried, Brad. It was just a silly faint. Let's go out and dance. I don't want to waste another moment.'

Charles Lafayette mopped his brow and followed them into the balmy night air. For one dreadful moment he'd thought the party he'd planned for so long was going to have to be abruptly curtailed. He reached for a cigar, the anxiety fading as he smoked it and watched Gussie laughingly reassure her friends as to her health, and dance joyfully with first Bradley, then Austin Merriweather, then Jason Shreve and then Bradley again.

The modern gyrations of the young gave way to rousing formation dances at which even he joined in. Gussie led the reels, hands clapping, eyes shining, swirling deftly with first one partner and then another. As the night hours merged into those of early dawn, the music slowed and closely clasped couples swayed together to the soft strains of Gershwin and Cole Porter, satin and silken hems trailing in the dew-wet grass.

Bradley kissed her lingeringly. 'It's bedtime, princess,' he said at last, raising his head from hers, his voice catching in his throat as he gazed down at the soft sensuous contours of her mouth, the shining mass of her hair and the dark depths of her eyes.

She smiled wickedly. 'Won't you join me?' she whispered.

There was a hot flush at the back of his eyes and his arms tightened around her so that she gasped in delight.

'Another two months, and you won't be able to tease me any longer, Augusta Lafayette. I'll have you wherever and whenever I please.'

She giggled, silencing him with her lips, feeling her spine melt and her bones turn to water. He could have her now, right there on the lawn if he wanted, and he knew it. The fact that he didn't do so only made her want him more. Sex with Bradley was going to be glorious and she had only until October to wait until they were married. She sighed, wishing that he wasn't quite so adamant about her retaining her virtue until then. He hadn't cared about Mae's virtue, or the virtue of the scores of other girls he had dated. But then, she reminded herself as they began to stroll hand in hand back to the house, he hadn't been in love with them. He hadn't wanted to marry them.

The fairy lights still gleamed in the trees, pale reflections now as the pearl-grey sky took on the first golden hints of dawn. Champagne corks littered the sweet-smelling grass. Down at the pool, her aunt and Jim Meredith and a score of others still laughed and danced. The band, bleary eyed, still played for the remaining couples.

Gussie sighed blissfully. It had been a perfect party. Nearly as perfect as her wedding day would be.

Bradley broke off a full-blown rose from the bank of flowers that fronted the porticoed entrance to the house and slid it into her hair so that it rested at her temple. She smiled; a gentle, soft, sensuous smile that caught at his heart.

In the marble-floored hallway a maid was waiting to usher her to her room and put her to bed.

'Are you coming in for breakfast?' she asked.

He shook his head. 'No, I'm going now. Ring me when you wake up.'

He kissed her one last time and she paused at the doorway, reluctant to go inside and lose sight of him. The moon faded in the glowing sky, the sun inched to the rim of the horizon. She leaned against a fluted pillar and dreamily removed the rose from her hair, smelling its fragrance, watching in a world of her own as Bradley strolled, broad-shouldered and handsome to his Thunderbird.

His parents had gone home long ago, carefully chauffered as the majority of guests had been. Her aunts and uncles, cousins and second-cousins were sleepily making their way to bed, or lingering over coffee and the hot buffet breakfast that was being served in the dining room and which her father was hosting. She could no longer see the band but she could hear the faint notes of a last waltz. Bradley's car disappeared down the oak-lined drive. She blew a kiss in its direction and turned to enter the house.

The shadow fell across her as softly as a kiss. She stood perfectly still, her heart hammering. This time she would not chase it away. This time she would know, once and for all. It enveloped her, caressing her so that she could hardly breathe.

'*Augusta, Augusta.*'

The very air seemed to whisper her name. She felt beads of perspiration break out on her forehead and her fingers tightened around the rose. Perhaps if she moved very slowly, perhaps this time . . . Almost imperceptibly she turned her head. The steps behind her were deserted. On the distant lawn two or three couples remained, locked in each other's arms, too distant to be recognizable. There was no one there: no one to be seen. With a low moan she fled into the house, the crushed petals of the rose scattering in her wake.

Charles Lafayette was buoyant. In the week following the party Augusta had been unusually quiet and had looked strained and tired – obviously Jim Meredith had been right about the excitement being too much for her – but now from the direction of the pool came the sound of records being played, and laughter. A smile tinged his mouth. A pool party. Augusta was once more feeling her usual vivacious self. He had seen the Shreve boys arrive with Bradley, and he had glimpsed Mae Jefferson and Austin Merriweather. He strolled towards his study, happy with his daughter's friends, happy with his daughter, happy with life. His cousin Leo was remaining at St Michel for a prolonged vacation before returning to Vancouver, as was the great aunt. It was wonderful to have family around again, and tonight Leo had promised him a treat.

★

'I like home movies, Cousin Leo. I won't be bored, honestly.'

Leo Lafayette smiled indulgently at her. 'Most of them are of Vancouver and of people you don't know. I thought they'd be of interest to your father, not you.'

'Well, they *do* interest me,' Augusta said. 'And you took some of my birthday party, didn't you?'

'Reels and reels.'

'Then we'll have another party tonight. A *family* party, and watch them. Aunt Tina is coming to supper and Great Aunt Belle is still with us. Daddy is afraid she isn't ever going to leave.'

Great Aunt Belle was as eager as Gussie to see the movies, as she announced later that evening when all was ready. 'Perhaps now we'll know what it is you *do* up in Canada,' she said grouchily, sitting herself in the centre of the sofa. 'No wife, no children. What sort of a life is that?'

Leo grinned and winked at Augusta, and Augusta winked back. She liked her Cousin Leo. Younger than her father, he had none of her father's austere manner. He had cut loose from New Orleans long ago, and his visits were always long looked-forward-to treats.

Tina sat gracefully beside Great Aunt Belle, displaying long, silken legs and sipping a glass of wine. Charles Lafayette nursed a glass of brandy and sat in a leather wing chair while Augusta perched on the arm.

'Goodness,' Augusta said as a girl little older than herself skied to a halt in front of the camera and blew a kiss. 'So *that* is what you get up to in Canada, Uncle Leo!'

There were roars of laughter and Great Aunt Belle made disapproving noises though her mouth twitched suspiciously at the corners.

'Oh, there's me,' Augusta cried, clapping her hands delightedly at the sight of herself in her Paris gown as she

81

greeted her guests, her father standing proudly on one side of her, Bradley on the other. 'Doesn't Bradley look handsome? Look, there's Eden flirting with him quite openly whenever I'm not looking. And there's Cousin Theobald with Mae and just *look* at the expression of his face! He obviously can't wait to get away.'

'There's Conrad Hampton. If Bradley still looks as good when he's his father's age, you will be a lucky girl,' Tina Lafayette purred.

Great Aunt Belle snorted in disapproval and Leo grinned. He knew very well the kind of tricks his little relative got up to.

'And there we are dancing,' Gussie said, clasping her hands around her knees, leaning forward. 'Doesn't my dress look divine? I shall keep it until I'm an old lady. There's Eden again, this time with Cousin Frederick. I never realized before what a flirt Eden is. And there's Austin Merriweather trying to dance and failing miserably. Poor Austin. All that money and no sex appeal. And there's Jason Shreve looking quite sophisticated in his tuxedo, and there's—'

The words choked in her throat, her eyes widened, the blood drained from her face.

'What is it, Gussie? Do you feel faint?' Tina asked, starting to her feet.

Leo left the projector flickering its laughing, dancing images on the screen and grabbed her shoulders.

'Gussie! Stop staring like that! Charles, I think she's gone into a trance!'

Charles Lafayette had been monentarily transfixed by shock. Now he pushed his brother away, seized his daughter and shook her. 'Gussie! *Gussie!*'

Slowly Gussie's eyes focused on her father's frightened face.

'Gussie, are you all right? What *is* it? Shall I call Dr Meredith? Tina, call Jim Meredith ...'

'No ...' Unsteadily Gussie rose to her feet. 'No ... I don't want to see anyone.' Dazedly her eyes were dragged back to the now blank screen.

'Let me put her to bed,' Tina Lafayette said practically. 'Send Allie up with a glass of hot milk, Charles. I'll give her two of my sleeping tablets and she'll be fine by morning.'

Slowly, like a sleep-walker, Gussie climbed the stairs to her room, holding on to the banisters as if at any second she would lose consciousness and fall crashing to the floor.

Charles and Leo looked at each other bewilderedly.

'Gussie's never been ... histrionic, has she?' Leo asked hesitantly as Gussie stumbled to her room.

Charles Lafayette wheeled on him, his face savage. 'Of course she hasn't! We'll have no such talk in this house! Gussie is perfectly normal. She's over-excited, that's all.' He mopped his sweating brow with a large silk handkerchief.

'Sorry, Charles. I wasn't insinuating ...'

'Forget it,' Charles Lafayette snapped. 'Tina is right. What Gussie needs is a good night's sleep.'

He rang for Allie and ordered the little maid to take a glass of hot milk immediately to Augusta. While he was doing so Leo thoughtfully rewound the film aware that he had been tactless in referring, however obliquely, to the skeleton in the family cupboard.

'It was just about here, Charles. There's Gussie dancing with Bradley,' he said easily, trying to make amends.

Unwillingly Charles Lafayette sat down and watched the re-run of his daughter's party.

'There's that friend of hers, Mae is it? There's the Merriweather boy dancing.'

Charles Lafayette's fingers tightened over the arm of his

chair. 'There's Jason Shreve,' he said, 'and there's – *My God!*'

Leo looked at his cousin in surprise. Charles's face was ashen, his eyes incredulous, fixed, as Gussie's had been, on the screen.

Leo turned swiftly to see what had caused such an outburst of shock. Gussie was dancing with Bradley, her face radiant, her hair spilling freely down her neck. The Merriweather boy was making awkward movements with his rosy-cheeked girlfriend. Jason Shreve was chatting up an older woman who should have known better. There were other dancers that Leo did not know. All young; all carefree. All enjoying themselves. In the distance were tiny groups composed mainly of New Orleans' more sedate citizens, chatting, champagne glasses in their hands. A maid was circulating with a silver tray of hors d'oeuvres; a waiter could be seen opening a bottle of champagne. Charles was on the film, his back to the dancers, his head bowed to hear what the small, elderly woman he was talking to was saying. Under the trees a girl that looked suspiciously like Desirée Ashington had her back to the camera, her arms around a young man's neck. Farther left, nearly out of the picture, another figure stood, watching intently, his face cast into darkness by the heavy foliage of the oak beneath which he was standing.

Leo stopped the film and re-ran it. There was nothing, absolutely nothing to cause such an expletive from his usually carefully-spoken cousin. At the point where Gussie had choked on her words and Charles had blasphemed, he halted the film.

'What is it, Charles? I can't see a damn thing wrong myself.'

Slowly Charles Lafayette rose to his feet. 'There!' he rasped, 'beneath the tree. Do you see?'

Leo looked. Desirée and her boyfriend were caught for all

time indiscreetly kissing. He shrugged. 'It was a little early, but so what? An hour later, everyone was kissing everyone else.'

'No, not them. *Him!*'

He stabbed at the dark figure beneath the oak. Leo looked from the film to his cousin and back again. Charles looked nearly as ill as Gussie had looked.

'I don't know him. Who is he?'

Charles did not answer for a long time. He stared at the frozen image and then said slowly, 'He *looks* like Beauregard Clay.'

'And would Beauregard Clay have been such a disastrous guest?' Leo asked, intrigued.

Charles laughed harshly. 'Beauregard Clay is dead. Gussie had a schoolgirl crush on him and she took his death pretty badly, for a time – until Bradley came along.'

Leo regarded the dark figure beneath the trees with interest. 'I see. No wonder the film gave her such a shock. But who *is* he? Beau's brother?'

'Beau Clay's brother is five foot three, fair-haired and lives in Houston. Only Judge Clay was at the party.'

Leo turned back to the film; the tense, intent figure beneath the trees was that of a young man, not an old man.

'Then who?' he asked. 'Your guest list was highly selective. Whom did you invite who resembles Beauregard Clay?'

'No one,' Charles Lafayette snapped. 'Not a damned soul,' he said and tearing his eyes from the screen strode white-lipped from the room.

Leo re-ran the film again, and the next film, and the next. Nearly the whole of Augusta's party was depicted at one stage or another. Face after face reappeared, but no matter how carefully he searched the screen he saw no resemblance to the faceless figure beneath the trees. Whoever he had been, he had not danced. That powerful, slim-hipped figure would have been immediately recognizable. Even caught motionless, there was a sense of power under restraint emanating from his body.

At last, tired and red-eyed from his efforts, Leo Lafayette switched off the projector and the lights in the room. Whoever he was, he had spoiled a nice evening. He was glad Bradley hadn't been there to see the extent of Gussie's reaction. Filled with a strange sense of foreboding, too restless for sleep, he lit a cigar and strolled out into the velvet blackness, gazing across the moonlit lawns to where the giant oak stood, its dark silhouette strangely menacing aginst the scudding clouds of the night sky.

CHAPTER FOUR

Gussie lay in her vast bed, her eyes wide, staring blankly at the ceiling. How could she have forgotten him so easily? That lithe body, that unmistakeable way of standing, deceptively at ease, yet as alert as the most dangerous of predators. She bit her bottom lip and tasted blood. She had wanted him and she had bound him to her forever. Sweat broke out on her forehead. She was being hysterical. The man beneath the trees had not been Beau. Beau was dead. Shrouded in his family's monolithic tomb. She had thought she had forgotten him. Her birthday party, her forthcoming wedding, Bradley, all had conspired to drive him from her mind, but now he was back in full force, her longing for him so intense it was a physical pain.

Gussie threw herself from the bed and paced the room, pressing her hands against her throbbing temple. 'Beau! Beau!' Unconsciously she called his name aloud, her voice anguished. Why had he died? Why had he not lived and come for her on that far-off night of Midsummer's Eve? She sat in the window seat, her tear-wet cheek pressed close to the glass as fireflies danced against the pane. If he had come for her she would have been marrying Beau in October. Beau with his hard glittering eyes and savage mouth; Beau with his indecent appetite for life and fearlessness and daring.

Despite the soft warmth of the night, she shivered in her lace-trimmed nightdress. She had been destined to marry Beau and now she was going to marry Bradley. She could barely remember Bradley's face. It was Beau's image that burned in her brain. She could see the narrow eyes set slanting above high cheekbones, the mouth quirking in a mocking smile as if he were only feet away from her.

'Oh my love,' she whispered as the moon rode high in the sky. 'Why did you leave me? Why? Why?'

Leo settled himself into Charles's leather wing chair and shook open a copy of the morning paper, thankful for his bachelorhood and his consequent lack of worries. The guest list for the party was on a side table, names scored through viciously in red ink. Though Charles had not told him when they'd met at breakfast, Leo knew that Charles had spent most of the night hours going over and over it, searching for the guest who bore an uncanny resemblance to the dead Beauregard Clay.

'Good morning, Cousin Leo. Has Daddy gone?'

Leo peered over the top of the centre page. 'About fifteen minutes ago, Gussie.' He frowned. Unless he was very much mistaken, Gussie's slender shoulders appeared to be relaxed, and it seemed to him that her lemon dress and matching hair ribbon were not the sort of clothes someone who was distressed might wear. It seemed that Charles had been overreacting to Gussie's behaviour the previous evening.

'Going somewhere special?' he asked with a smile.

'I'm having lunch with Bradley. There's a house at Baton Rouge he wants us to have a look at.'

'That young man certainly doesn't let the grass grow under his feet, does he?'

Gussie gave a small smile. 'No. Would you like some more coffee, Cousin Leo?'

'I wouldn't say no. I've lived in Vancouver so long, I've forgotten how good real chicory coffee tastes.'

Gussie rang for Allie and then sat on the sofa, staring towards the far corner of the room where the screen had stood the night before. She had made up her eyes and her lips were glossed, but her face was pale, her eyes pensive.

'I thought perhaps Bradley would be tempted by the North,' Leo said, injecting a note of briskness into his voice in an effort to dispel her sombre quietness. 'New York or Washington, for instance.'

Allie came in with the coffee and Gussie poured.

'No. Bradley is a Southerner through and through. He wants to stay here and build up a law practice.'

Leo's eyebrows rose. 'I thought Bradley was all set to take over the family's banking fortunes?'

With an effort, Gussie tore her eyes away from the corner of the room. 'He wants to make it on his own first. That's why he wants to buy a place instead of renting one or living at St Michel or with his parents.'

Leo sipped at his coffee. 'As I remember it, the Hampton home would house an army. It must be one of the biggest plantation houses left in the district.' He shook his head, thinking of his neat service flat in Vancouver. 'Why people still want to live on in those great white mausoleums, I can't imagine.'

Gussie trembled so violently that her coffee spilled into the saucer. Mausoleums. She had never visited the Clay mausoleum. She had never paid her respects. She set the cup and saucer down unsteadily. Perhaps she should go. Perhaps she should make an excuse to Bradley and go today. She heard the Thunderbird sweep to a halt outside St Michel's entrance with a screech of tyres.

'Have a nice day,' Leo said, returning to his paper.

'Yes ...' It was too late now. She could already hear Bradley's voice greeting the butler. She would go tomorrow: or the day after.

'Hello, princess,' Bradley said, taking her in his arms and kissing her full on the mouth. 'You look sensational.'

89

She clung to him, relief flooding through her. This was Bradley: flesh and blood: warm and loving. Suddenly her fears seemed groundless, and her melancholia lifted. She was going to view a house that could well be her future home. She was happy and in love.

Hands clasped, they ran down St Michel's wide shallow steps and towards the car. As Bradley swung the door open for her, a small exhalation of breath brushed the nape of her neck. She halted, trying to keep hold of the sensation, but it vanished as swiftly as it had come.

'What is it, sweetheart?'

'Nothing.' She got into the car and Bradley started the engine.

'Bradley . . .' She hesitated. She wanted to tell him. She wanted to share everything with him only it was so difficult. They eased out of the drive and the Thunderbird picked up speed. 'Bradley, last night the strangest thing happened.'

'Your father got stoned.'

'No.' For once her usual giggle was absent. 'Cousin Leo was showing some film of my birthday party and . . .'

'Idiot.' Bradley said as a pale blue Continental swerved out in front of him. 'What were you saying, honey? Were they good?'

'Yes.' Her voice was bleak. 'Yes. They were very good.'

She couldn't tell Bradley. He would laugh at her; tease her. Besides, she didn't really *want* to tell Bradley. She wanted to keep her thoughts of Beau Clay to herself.

'It's plenty big enough,' Bradley said as he and Gussie strolled through the empty rooms. 'The pool isn't Olympic sized, but I like the way it's been landscaped with palms and magnolias. What do you think of the balcony off the main bedroom? We can breakfast there and pretend we're in the Vieux Carré.'

'It's lovely, Brad,' she said softly, her voice holding none of its usual verve.

Bradley frowned and stared down at her. 'You don't have to like it to please me, Gussie. I don't care *where* we live as long as you are happy.'

She forced a smile and squeezed his hand. 'I mean it, Brad. It's lovely.'

Faintly perturbed, Bradley led the way back to the car and drove to the nearest restaurant.

'Are you feeling O.K., Gussie?' he asked as the waiter took their order. 'You look pale.'

'I'm fine. Truly.'

Bradley wondered if being faced with the house had given her a sudden attack of pre-wedding nerves. Instead of laughing and chattering, squeezing his arm, kissing him at every opportunity, teasing him unmercifully, Gussie remained strangely subdued, barely hearing him when he spoke to her. The day was not turning out remotely as he had envisaged. Instead of Gussie being overjoyed at the sight of their future home, she seemed almost indifferent. Instead of the happy celebration he had planned, she was picking listlessly at her food and ignoring the expensive wine he had selected with such care.

Her mood was contagious. By the end of the meal he, too, had lapsed into silence, though Gussie seemed unaware of it.

Disappointedly he drove her home, hoping that the sight of St Michel would arouse her from her stupor and that she would ask why they had returned so soon. She didn't. She allowed him to kiss her goodbye and then said hesitantly, 'Do you believe that love is forever, Bradley?'

He tilted her chin so that her troubled eyes met his. 'Of course, I do, darling. I shall never love anyone else. Is that what's been troubling you?' He grinned and held her close.

'Goose,' he said tenderly. 'How could you ever imagine that I would cease to love you?'

A faint frown puckered her brow. 'Once you give your word there can be no going back, can there?'

'Never.' He held her close, trying to reassure her foolish doubts.

Her face was pressed against his chest. She said indistinctly, 'Then it isn't possible to love again when you have already vowed your love to someone else?'

'No.' He held her away from him, his voice emphatic. 'I don't know what's got into you, Gussie, but I can tell you that I've never loved anyone else and that I never *will* love anyone else. When we make our wedding vows I intend to keep them. Understand?'

'Yes.' Her voice was little more than a whisper, her eyes on his but strangely unseeing and unfocussing. 'Yes,' she repeated. 'I understand.'

'Then stop looking so tragic and get back in the car. I've tickets for the theatre tonight.'

She shook her head. 'I'd rather not, Bradley. I don't feel too good. Maybe another night.'

'But the tickets are for tonight ...' he began and then stopped in mid-sentence. She was already halfway into the house.

'What the hell ...' he said and then savagely tore up the tickets and drove to a club in the French Quarter where he drank Hurricanes until his frustration was drowned in an alcoholic haze.

Gussie sat on her bed and stared at her row of dolls. The dolls stared back unblinkingly. Why did she feel so strange? Why had she hurt Bradley when he had made so much effort to make the day special? Why could she not give him her attention? Why was it centred so firmly on Beau Clay?

Slowly she moved across to the dressing table and sat

down. Did she love Beau, and not Bradley? Did she love them both? Or did she love Bradley, and did Beau know, and was his presence at her side a reminder of her foolishness; of her lightly-made vow? She slammed down the hair brush so hard on the polished wood that it splintered. She was being idiotic. There were no such things as ghosts. Beau was dead and had never loved her. That had all been in her imagination. She was in love with Bradley; she was going to marry Bradley. She was bound to no one else but the man whose ring she wore on the third finger of her left hand.

'*Forever*,' the silence breathed. '*Forever and forever and forever.*'

'No!' she shouted, drowning the insidious whisper. 'It was a *game*! It didn't mean anything! It couldn't have!'

'*Forever*.' The words echoed and reverberated. Vainly she pressed her hands over her ears. Bradley had believed that once a vow was given it could not be broken. She had vowed to make Beau Clay love her forever. Was he surmounting death to keep his promise? Was it Beau's shadow that fell across her on the cloudiest of days? Beau's voice that whispered so insistently in her ear? Beau, who had stood beneath the trees of St Michel and watched in jealous anger as she danced with another man?

She groaned, scarcely recognizing herself in the glass. Her eyes seemed huge in her whitened face. The gaiety and the vivacity had gone. All that was left was a mental anguish that grew steadily, minute by minute. She closed her eyes, fighting for self-control. She had to think. She had to behave rationally. Eden: she would telephone Eden. Eden's commonsense was unfailing.

With shaking hands she dialled the Alexanders' number.

'Hi! Nice to hear from you at last,' Eden said, putting *Madame Bovary* down and pouring herself another glass of chilled Chablis.

93

'Can you come over, Eden? Now?'

At the tone of her voice, Eden paused, holding the bottle in mid-air. 'What is it Gussie? You sound ill.'

'I'm not ill. I just need to talk and I can't do it over the phone. Please come.'

'I'm on my way.' Eden recorked the Chablis, flung it into her bag and walked quickly from the room. Gussie's time had been so taken up with Bradley that she hadn't seen her in ages. However, one thing was for sure. The voice on the phone had not been that of the old, fun-loving, irrepressible Gussie.

'My God,' Eden said as she entered Gussie's bedroom. 'I thought future brides were supposed to be radiant. You look like Mae on a bad night.'

'Quit joking, Eden. I feel terrible.'

'I believe you,' Eden said, searching for a tooth mug and filling it with Chablis. 'You look it. What's wrong?'

Gussie sat on the edge of the bed and stared at her. Now that it had come to it, the whole thing sounded so ridiculous that she didn't know where to begin.

'Here.' Eden handed her the tooth mug and searched for another glass. 'I've discovered a delicious fact of life. I'm an alcoholic who never gets drunk.'

Gussie sipped the wine. Eden sat on the window seat and waited. At last Gussie said awkwardly, 'Do you remember that silly ritual we held here the night Beau Clay died?'

Imperceptibly Eden stiffened. 'Yes. What of it?'

'It couldn't have *meant* anything, could it?'

'In what way?'

Gussie felt her throat tighten with suppressed hysteria. 'Well, it couldn't have *worked*, could it?'

Eden shrugged. '*You* thought it could.'

Gussie put her glass down and hugged her arms around her body as if she were cold. 'But Beau died.'

'Yes.' Eden regarded Gussie curiously.

Gussie rose from the bed and began to pace the room, rubbing her arms as if to bring some warmth back into them.

'Eden, I think I'm going mad. I keep hearing Beau calling my name. I keep feeling his shadow. Today I felt his breath on the nape of my neck!'

Eden tried to check her, but once started Gussie rushed on heedlessly.

'He was at my birthday party! Cousin Leo took movies and he was there, on the film! I swear he was! He doesn't want me to marry Bradley! He wants me for himself! He's going to love me forever, just as I said he would!'

Eden sprang from the window seat and grabbed her, halting her frenzied pacing. 'You're *hysterical*, Augusta Lafayette. Beau Clay is dead.'

'Then he wants me to join him! He wants us to be together!'

Eden slapped her viciously across the face and Gussie collapsed on to the floor, sobbing unrestrainedly.

'I loved him so much,' she gasped. 'I would have sold my soul to have had him. Is that what I've done, Eden? Sold my soul?'

'Your sanity more like,' Eden said cruelly, dragging her to her feet and shaking her. 'That childish charade was utterly meaningless, Gussie. If you hear Beau Clay calling your name it's because subconsciously you want to hear him call your name. It's about time you put him from your mind. You loved him and he's dead. Now you love Bradley. Be careful with that glass of wine. It's a nineteen seventy-one.'

Gussie fought for breath. 'Do you mean it, Eden? Is it my imagination?'

95

'Undoubtedly.'

'But the movie!'

'The world and his brother were at St Michel that night. No doubt someone who resembled Beau was there. I made an ass of myself in Goldberg's yesterday. I thought it was Dean being served at the counter and rushed in, covering his eyes and chirrupping "Guess who?". It turned out to be a tourist from England.'

'What did you do?' Gussie's breathing was returning to normal. She wiped her eyes and reached for the tooth mug.

'Had a most enjoyable evening,' Eden said with a grin.

Gussie laughed tremulously.

'If I'm going to be your bridesmaid, we ought to decide definitely about colours for the dress. I refuse to wear pastels. Mae, as your maid-of-honour, would look fine, but I would look as if I'd just stepped off the top of a Christmas cake.'

'Well, you can't wear scarlet!' Gussie said, giggling, feeling as if the world had righted on its axis. 'Where did you get that outfit from, Eden? It's incredible.'

Eden looked down at her crushed velvet, searing red jacket and culottes and said calmly, 'It was one of the costumes for that last Shakespearian production at college. I just altered it a little here and there. It's rather stunning, don't you think?'

'It's different,' Gussie said truthfully and agreed to Eden's suggestion that they go out to eat. The dark weight that seemed at times to crush her had evaporated. She felt happy; normal; sane.

Later in the evening she rang Bradley to apologize for her behaviour and to tell him how thrilled she was with the house. In the days that followed they saw each other constantly, went swimming, to restaurants, for walks in the park. She didn't turn, or even hesitate in their conversation when the dark, cold shadow fell across her path. Instead she chatted more brightly, laughed more loudly. Her brittle gaiety was overpowering.

Bradley sensed her underlying fear and asked her time and time again if she wanted to postpone the wedding. The prospect only made her more excitable. She wanted to marry him: today, tomorrow. As soon as possible.

'Another death for the Clays,' her father said as they breakfasted together a few weeks later. 'Not that this is the tragedy young Beau's death was. Judge Clay's mother was eighty-four at least.'

Gussie had been about to reach for a slice of toast. Her hand fell into her lap; the blood drained from her face.

'Laetitia Clay,' Charles Lafayette said, removing his spectacles and folding up the newspaper. 'She was quite a lady in her youth. I believe she had a soft spot for Beau, for all his wildness.' He rose to his feet. 'The funeral is on Friday, Gussie. Tell Allie to make sure your dark clothes are ready.'

'No!' She pushed her chair away from the table. '*No!* I'm not going!'

Her father's steel-grey eyebrows rose imperceptibly. It was not often he was firm with Augusta. 'Laetitia Clay was one of the oldest and most respected of New Orleans' citizens. Judge Clay is a personal friend of mine. I expect you to accompany me, Gussie.'

Gussie stared after him, appalled. When her father spoke in that tone there was no arguing with him. She began to shake. She remembered clearly the burials she'd had to attend before. The hideous depositing of the body on the stone shelf. The mouldering, swathed bodies on other shelves. The smell of death and decay. When the Clay family tomb was opened there would be another brief glimpse of the long dead; and of the not-so-long dead. She raised a hand to her mouth and stifled a cry. In the last few weeks only Eden had saved her sanity. With utter conviction, Eden had repeated time and again that the presence at her side, the voice she heard at all times of the day and night, was nothing but her imagination. She was *not* insane. She was *not* possessed. She was sensitive and overwrought and had reacted badly to the death of a man she had idolized. Like a litany, Gussie had repeated Eden's words until she had almost come to believe them. *Had* believed them when Bradley was at her side and the room was crowded and the music loud. Now she would be faced with a nightmare: the sight of Beau's dead body: the terrible knowledge that he still held her heart and that Bradley had never completely succeeded him. She hated Laetitia Clay for dying. She hated her father for imposing his will on her. Most of all, she hated herself for not being able to love Bradley as he deserved.

The heat was oppressive, the sky overcast as the mourners followed the coffin to the old, overgrown graveyard in the centre of New Orleans. Gussie squeezed her hands together tightly. The St Louis Cemetery was itself a city. A city of the dead. How could Beau have been laid to rest in such overpowering grimness? How could he have borne it?

The priest held up his arm and blessed the assembly as they halted before the ornate magnificence of the Clay mausoleum.

'Dearly beloved. We are gathered here today to pay our respects to one of our most revered citizens. A lady of great character; great fortitude . . .'

The iron grille before the mausoleum was still closed, the officiants standing by, ready to open it. Gussie tried to tear her eyes away, and could not.

'I have seen death too often to believe in death ... To be mortal is to share in divinity ...'

Beads of sweat broke out on Gussie's brow. If she fainted her father would have to carry her from the graveyard. She felt queasy. There was a tight band around her chest. Judge Clay's sister was crying softly.

'Come to meet her, angels of the Lord. Welcome her. Present her to God, the most high. Saints of God, come to her aid ...'

The same words had rung over Beau's coffin. Beau, too, had lain shrouded and still on that high catafalque.

'I am the resurrection, the truth and the light ...'

She should never have come. She should have defied her father.

'May the angels speed you into Paradise, and the Masters welcome you as you draw near and lead you into Jerusalem, the Heavenly City ...'

Gussie swayed. Was it never going to end? The sound of sobs intensified. Laetitia Clay had been well-loved.

'Lord, grant her everlasting rest and let perpetual light shine upon her. May she rest in peace. Amen.'

The grille was swung open. The priest was sprinkling holy water on the mummified body in the coffin. Gussie's heart began to slam against her chest in thick, heavy strokes. She would not look when the last barrier to the interior of the tomb was removed. She would remember him as he was; standing beneath the tree, watching with jealous passion as she danced in Bradley's arms. Her hands were clammy, her breath coming shallow and fast. Beau had been dead when she had danced at her birthday party. Dead as Laetitia Clay was dead.

Judge Clay stepped forward and sprinkled holy water on the body of his mother, his face haggard. His sister and son followed.

'*Augusta. Augusta.*'

She gave a small cry, staring round her with petrified eyes. Her father's fingers tightened on her arm. Augusta had not been close to Laetitia Clay. There was no need for her to express undignified grief.

'*I'm here, Augusta,*' the barely audible voice said, floating up and around her. '*Forever and forever . . .*'

'Dead! Dead! Dead!' she chanted silently to herself, clinging desperately to a last shred of sanity. 'You're dead and I'm alone . . .'

The corpse was lifted from its casket. The heavy inner door of the mausoleum was opened slowly.

Gussie summoned up a remnant of courage. She would take one last, swift look; say one silent goodbye.

There were cries of incredulity and horror. Sobs rose to hysteria. Frenzied explanations were relayed to those at the back who had no view of the tomb. The priest faltered in his task. Laetitia's body was held aloft, rudely jostled by those who pushed forward to see for themselves.

The stone shelf that had held the body of Beau Clay was empty. Only other, older grey mounds of disintegrating bodies waited to be joined by Laetitia Clay.

'Oh my God! It isn't possible! It's gone, I tell you! Gone!'

Pandemonium broke out and Laetitia Clay's body was ignored. The priest was ashen-faced. A flashbulb popped boldly. Dignity was dispensed with. Revered members of the community fought for a vantage point. Screams and sobs echoed round the grim monoliths of the dead.

The priest was the first to recover his equilibrium, and he tersely ordered the bearers of Laetitia's body to deposit her inside the tomb as quickly as possible. With indecent haste, the inner door was slammed into place, the iron grille following.

'Who would want to do such a terrible thing?'

'Is it a joke? Have those wild friends of Beau's taken his body as a joke?'

'Some joke. How the hell would they get in there? It's sealed as tightly as a Hampton bank!'

Charles Lafayette caught his daughter as she fell. This time there was no Bradley to carry her with swift ease. The crowd pushed in, milling and shouting. Charles glimpsed Judge Clay's stunned, uncomprehending face and then he was pushing his way frantically through the mass of near-hysterical bodies. Twice he stumbled, but there was no one to come to his assistance. No one had time for anything but speculation as to what had happened to the body of Beauregard Clay.

The Lafayette chauffeur had been lolling against the bonnet of the limousine reading the *States Item*. As Charles Lafayette staggered from the graveyard, Augusta in his arms, the chauffeur dropped the paper to the pavement and ran to his employer, taking the insensible weight of the girl.

Charles Lafayette's face was grey. 'Home! Fast! Must ring Jim Meredith!'

The chauffeur laid Gussie on the rear seat and her father practically scrambled into the car. 'For Christ's sake, man! Move!'

Charles Lafayette twisted round in his seat, reaching a hand out to steady Gussie. Her face was marble-white; her eyelids were closed.

'Of all the tasteless, vulgar, barbaric acts,' Charles said to Jim Meredith as he closed Gussie's bedroom door behind them.

Jim Meredith shook his head. 'It's hard to credit, Charles. Are you sure Beau's body was not simply on a shelf other than the one people expected?'

'The only remains in that tomb had been there for thirty years or more,' Charles said firmly, pouring two stiff brandies. 'The body had been taken all right, and I can imagine by whom.'

Jim Meredith waited. He had never seen Charles so distressed before. 'Those hellrakes young Clay used to associate with. It would be their idea of a joke. They're sick. Promiscuous, Marxist and sick. The shock nearly killed Augusta.'

'Augusta's fine,' Jim Meredith said soothingly. 'Obviously she's deeply shocked. It's a pity you were right up front with the family mourners, but it can't be helped. She's young. She'll soon forget.'

'They deserve tarring and feathering when they're caught,' Charles Lafayette said viciously. 'Prison's too good for them. I'd whip their hides myself, given the chance.'

A flicker of amusement lit Jim Meredith's eyes. Charles Lafayette was the mildest mannered man he knew. Nothing but distress to Augusta could have aroused such passion.

'They'll find them,' he said reassuringly. 'Judge Clay will see to that. If the body has been taken – and I must say, Charles, that I'm still not one hundred per cent convinced of the fact – then the Clay family will go to every length to see that it is returned.'

'*If* they find it,' Charles Lafayette said, sinking into his chair, feeling suddenly old. 'You should have heard the inane babbling of the Delatours and Lafittes. It took them all of two seconds to come to the conclusion that the body had been taken for use in a black magic ceremony. We're going to hear nothing in this town but voodoo and witchcraft for the next six months.'

Jim Meredith's face was stern. 'Then see that Gussie doesn't get to hear any such foolish talk. Warn Bradley. He'll see to it that she isn't exposed to such idiocy. I like that boy. He's got both charm and sense. A rare combination.'

Alone in her vast bed Augusta lay motionless. Where was he, her dead lover? His voice was silent now, his presence absent. She wondered: if she held out her arms, if she pleaded with him to come and take her, if she, too, would die, his kiss on her lips, his arms around her as their spirits soared. Beneath the silken sheets she dug her nails into her palms, resisting the temptation. Beau would not want her to die. She was eighteen. The whole of her life stretched before her. Her forehead burned. It had stretched before Beau, too. When she had summoned his heart to hers he had attempted to reach her in such desperate haste that he had killed himself. That was how Beau had died. She knew it as surely as she knew his body no longer inhabited the Clay mausoleum.

A pair of narrow eyes, slanting above high cheekbones, swam before her. His black hair had a blue sheen, his mouth curved into a smile. 'Beau,' she whispered, her hands sliding up and free of the sheets. 'Beau, my darling . . .'

'—Jim Meredith says you should take one of these three times a day for the next week or so,' her father said, striding into the room, a bottle of Valium in his hand.

She blinked, scarcely recognizing him, the vision shattered.

'Maybe we should take a vacation? Go down to Barbados or Antigua?'

'No, Daddy. I want to stay here.'

Close to Beau: close to the arms and lips that were just a fingertips' touch away.

Charles Lafayette thought he understood. It was not long now until the wedding and it was understandable that she would not wish to be parted from Bradley. He watched as she obediently swallowed a tablet, and then kissed her on the forehead. His little girl. She would be a wife soon. Bradley would take care of her.

When the door closed behind him, Gussie waited expectantly but the room remained as it had always been: the row of dolls lined the sofa; the late afternoon sun streamed through the window and on to the pale carpet and the array of perfumes and cosmetics on her dressing table. He did not come to her. She closed her eyes and slept.

'My mother nearly died of heart failure,' Eden said as she sat with Mae in one of their favourite haunts in the French Quarter. 'Who would do such a hideous thing?'

Mae shook her head unhappily and toyed with her absinthe frappe. 'Judge Clay has offered a reward of one hundred thousand dollars for information leading to the return of Beau's body,' she said, her eyes fixed on her drink.

'If the voodooists have got him, there's no money in the world will buy him back,' Eden said frankly. 'What does your grandmother think, Mae? Have you spoken with her?'

Mae shook her head vehemently. 'No, and I don't want to talk about it, either.'

Eden lapsed into silence. She had lived in New Orleans for only three years but she had heard plenty of strange talk about Mae's grandmother, about the voodoo that was still practised secretly. Still, if Mae didn't want to talk about it, she had no intention of forcing her.

It was Mae who broke the silence, saying hesitantly, 'Strange things *do* happen, Eden, though, don't they? Do you remember Midsummer's Eve? I know you laughed at me at the time, but I'm sure Gussie saw more in that mirror than she ever let on.'

'Rubbish.' Eden's voice had a tight edge to it.

'She's never been quite the same since.'

'But that's because Beau died, not because of the ceremony.'

'That's the point.' The blood had drained from Mae's rosy face. 'Beau Clay died the night Gussie bound him to her forever.'

They stared at each other and then Mae began to cry. 'I can't bear it, Eden. I'm sure something terrible is going to happen to Gussie. Just like it did to her grandmother.'

Eden's sleek brows met in a frown. 'What happened to Gussie's grandmother?'

Mae sobbed and struggled from the table. 'She went crazy and drowned herself. They said she was obsessed. Obsessed as Gussie is obsessed!' Before Eden could restrain her, Mae had pushed past startled customers and fled into the street.

Eden paid for the drinks and rose to her feet. Poor Gussie. A mother who died when she was born and a grandmother who had committed suicide. She wandered out into the strong sunlight. Down the street black musicians were playing exuberantly in the humid afternoon heat. The news of Beau's missing body would have hit Gussie hard. She opened the door of her Cadillac and started the engine. She was supposed to be seeing Dean at two o'clock but he wouldn't mind if she was late. She would call in at St Michel and see Gussie first.

Gussie was sitting on the porch swing, swinging listlessly. She showed no surprise, pleasure or disappointment at Eden's appearance.

'Hi,' Eden said, and perched herself on a pile of cushions. 'How's the happy bride?'

Gussie shrugged.

'If you keep on losing weight so rapidly, your wedding dress will never fit.'

'It's already been taken in twice.'

'I'm not surprised. I'm going to look gigantic in comparison. I like my dress, though. That deep lavender blue is soft without being too wishy-washy ...'

'You were wrong.'

Eden stared at her.

'You were wrong about Beau.' Her voice was flat and expressionless. 'He does love me. He does want me. He watches me all the time. He's watching me now – there, down by the cherry trees.'

'For Christ's sake!' Eden's face was aghast. 'Have you told anyone else this? You need a doctor, Gussie. A shrink.'

A slight smile tinged Gussie's mouth as she continued swinging. 'No, I don't. I'm not mad. I loved him and I wanted him and now he won't let me go.'

'Does Bradley know?' Eden felt the words strangle in her throat. Of course Bradley didn't know. He would have done something about it if he had.

'No. He wouldn't believe me even if I told him.'

'Neither do I,' Eden said firmly. 'You're letting Beau Clay obsess you. It's unhinging your mind, Gussie. You've got to stop it now: this minute.'

Gussie's eyes moved reluctantly from the distant cherry trees and rested unnervingly on Eden. 'You thought it was my imagination, didn't you Eden? Do you think it is my imagination that Beau is no longer in his family's tomb?'

'No, of course I don't. Whatever has happened to Beau's body is hideous, but not supernatural. Graves have been robbed before. I daresay if it wasn't for the fact that Beau was so well-known, we'd have hardly have heard about it.'

Gussie smiled a small, secret smile and Eden knew that she didn't believe her.

'What about the wedding? Are you going ahead with it?'

'Of course.' Gussie's voice was mildly surprised. 'I love

106

Bradley as well. It's just that I can't remember Bradley's face when he isn't with me. Not like I can Beau's. Beau's face is with me all the time.' Her eyes returned to the cherry trees. 'But I can't marry Beau, can I? Not unless I die, and I don't want to die.'

Eden rose unsteadily to her feet, thoroughly frightened. 'You're sick, Gussie. Beau Clay is dead. He doesn't love you: he never did.'

'Then why won't he free me?' Gussie demanded, her eyes burning with sudden intensity.

'I guess it's because you're always thinking of him,' Eden said awkwardly. 'Once you're married to Bradley you'll forget all about Beau Clay.'

'Yes.' The passion drained from her voice, leaving it as flat and expressionless as before. 'Yes. Once I marry Bradley, then everything will be all right.'

They were sitting on the edge of the dunes, the ocean shimmering beneath the heat of the sun.

'You *can't* have Jason Shreve as your best man,' Gussie said, laughing, her head resting against Bradley's shoulder. 'Daddy is determined that this wedding is going to be the social occasion of the year.'

'Jason Shreve is my closest friend,' Bradley said, relieved to see that the pallor of the last few weeks had fled, and that her eyes had regained their natural sparkle.

'Maybe, but the Shreves are ... well ...' She giggled. '... just the Shreves, I guess. Daddy would want you to have someone more prestigious.'

'Whose wedding is this?' Bradley asked, his hand slipping beneath her blouse and touching the warm softness of her flesh. 'Ours, or your father's?'

'Ours,' she said dreamily, allowing herself to be pushed gently back against the sand, her lips parting willingly as

Bradley's sought hers. His weight pinioned her, his body heavy against her.

Her hand slid pleasurably across the strong muscles of his back and up into the thickness of his hair. The curls sprang against her palm and her fingers tightened.

'I do love you, Bradley. You do believe me, don't you?'

There was a strange urgency in her voice. He raised his head and looked down at her: at her gentle, soft, sensuous mouth. At the tumbled, dishevelled mass of her wheat-gold hair. At her eyes, as velvet and dark as the heart of an exotic flower.

'You'd better do, Augusta Lafayette,' he said fiercely, the heat naked at the back of his eyes. 'Who else would you be in love with?'

Something indefinable crossed Augusta's face, to be instantly chased away. She loved Bradley. She was marrying Bradley. She was normal and sane and her marriage would prove it.

'No one,' she sighed passionately, pulling his head down to hers, her tongue flicking past his, searching, giving, desire flaring up in her.

He responded passionately, but then, just as she thought that he had lost his self-control, he grasped her wrists, pinning them high above her head, and said hoarsely, 'Not yet, Gussie. Not yet.'

She sobbed in anguish, and as he released her, clung to him in desperate need. If only Bradley would make love to her, then she could never belong to anyone else. Not ever.

'One week,' Bradley said, pulling her gently to her feet, cradling her in his arms. 'Then we'll be Mr and Mrs Hampton and honeymooning in Acapulco.'

'A week is a long time,' she said as they began to walk along the creaming shoreline. 'It seems like ...' She stopped. 'Forever' was a word she never uttered. Not to Bradley. Not since her birthday party. 'It seems like a lifetime,' she said, suddenly cold despite the shimmering heat of the midday sun.

CHAPTER FIVE

'Gussie, you look absolutely breathtaking,' Eden said as she adjusted the gardenias in her hair and gazed in blatant admiration at her friend.

Tina Lafayette was busily smoothing the French lace that billowed from Gussie's waist over a mass of petticoats, while Mae languished happily on Gussie's bed, watching the goings on with vicarious pleasure, thoughts of Austin never far from her mind. Gussie's neckline was heartshaped, the sleeves long and mediaevally pointed over the backs of her hands. Her headdress was made of roses and seed-pearls and the shoulder-length veil was thrown back from her face, falling lightly over her gleaming, silken hair. She looked like a princess from a fairy tale.

'Do you think a little more mascara?' Gussie asked Eden tentatively.

'No. Brides are supposed to look pure and unadorned. Your make-up is just right.'

There was a hint of shadow on Gussie's lids, a soft pink gloss on her lips. Her nails were unpolished, buffed to a pearly sheen. There was twenty minutes to go before she became Mrs Bradley Hampton.

She moved to sit down on the bed and Eden and Tina rushed forward, smoothing her skirts behind her.

'I think I'd like a drink of water, Cousin Tina,' she said, hands clasped lightly in her lap.

'I had champagne at my first wedding,' Tina Lafayette said, pouring out a wineglass of iced Perrier water. 'Both before and after the ceremony.' Her eyes danced wickedly. 'At my second wedding I had gin and giggled when I made my vows. Conrad never forgave me. He spent my wedding night telling me I was a lush.'

Eden grinned. She liked Tina Lafayette and was tempted to ask what she had drunk at her third wedding. And her fourth. She restrained herself. Now was not the time and place to ask.

Gussie took the wineglass from Tina, her hands trembling so violently that droplets sprinkled her gown.

'Good heavens, child! You'll mark the lace! Quick, Eden. Tissues.'

Hastily the droplets were blotted and Tina said, 'My, you are in a state of nerves, aren't you? I've never seen a bride so edgy.'

'I'm fine. Really I am.' Her voice was taut, belying her words.

'I hope so, honey. This is going to be the biggest wedding New Orleans has seen.'

Eden stood a foot or two away from them and regarded Gussie with faint apprehension. For the past few weeks Gussie had returned to apparent normality. She had made no further reference to Beau Clay and though she had lost more weight and was even more subdued, Eden had ceased to worry. Now she was assailed by doubts. Gussie had shown a strange inability to cope in stressful or over-exciting situations: at her birthday party she had fainted before half the town. She had done so again at Laetitia Clay's funeral. Today she would be exposed to hundreds of eyes. The cathedral would be packed. Photographers would impede her way from limousine to cathedral door.

The knot of apprehension grew. If Gussie fainted, the occasion would be recorded by every Louisiana newspaper. The most important event of her life would be marred: her

111

father would have to endure cruel gossip as to the bride's physical condition; Bradley would be distressed. Eden knew she should speak to Gussie but could not while Tina Lafayette and Mae remained with them.

Eden moved away and sat at the dressing table, applying blusher to her already perfect cheekbones. Her hand halted in mid-air. So Gussie had sat on Midsummer's Eve, her hair a golden cloud, her eyes glowing. Slowly she put the make-up brush down. *Had* Gussie believed she had seen Beau Clay through the mirror as she had sat so still while they whooped and cheered at her dramatic prank? She had never said so, but she had said things far more disturbing: that the ceremony had worked and that she had bound Beau Clay to her forever. If Mae had said the same thing, Eden would have laughed it off, but Gussie had been too adamant to have her statement so easily dismissed.

When Beau Clay's body had vanished from his tomb, Gussie had been near-deranged, believing that it was because he was searching for her: waiting for her. The nape of Eden's neck prickled. What was it Gussie had said? 'I can't marry Beau, not unless I die, and I don't want to die.' What had she meant by such an extraordinary statement? More to the point, if she believed what she said, and Eden knew without a shadow of a doubt that she did, what effect would such belief have on her mental health?

'Only another fifteen minutes, honey,' Tina Lafayette said gaily, fluffing her shoulder-length bob so that it would look devastating beneath her ridiculously tiny hat of rose petals. 'I'll go down and check on your father. He's been pacing the main salon as if it were his wedding day, not yours.'

'Oh – the bouquets,' Eden said quickly. 'Do you think you could check on them, Mae?'

The doors closed behind them, the fragrance of *Je Reviens* wafting in the draft.

112

'O.K., Gussie?' Eden asked.

'Yes.' Gussie's voice was steady, but the pre-wedding gaiety had vanished with Tina Lafayette.

'If there's anything bothering you, for goodness' sake tell me now,' Eden said, swinging to face her, her eyes concerned.

'No, nothing . . .' Gussie avoided Eden's eyes. She would marry Bradley, whom she loved, and then everything would be all right. The voices would stop: the shadows would disappear. Only another fifteen minutes. She couldn't tell Eden: Eden didn't believe her. Eden thought she was mad. She couldn't tell anybody: she didn't need to. Soon she would be Bradley's wife. The spell she had cast would be broken.

'Eden, sweetie, Mae says your bouquet is waiting downstairs . . .' Tina burst into the room, happily oblivious of any undercurrent. 'Your father is waiting for you, Gussie. We should arrive at the cathedral exactly five minutes late, which is just perfect. A bride should never be early . . . it smacks of eagerness. Now, where did I put my handkerchief? I'm bound to cry. I always do at weddings.'

She snatched up an infinitesimal wisp of lace with her initials lavishly embroidered on one corner. 'I must go down to your father, Gussie. He's been suddenly having second thoughts, saying that you're too young. Silly man. He just can't bear the thought of your being a wife as well as a daughter.' She whirled from the room and Eden, after giving Gussie another searching glance, followed her.

Gussie was alone. Slowly she rose from the bed and crossed to the dressing table. She sat down and stared at herself in the mirror. At herself and beyond. He was absent. She felt a sudden rush of tears to her eyes. Had he already left her? So soon? The pain was almost more than she could bear.

'I would have married you, my love,' she whispered to the

113

mirror that stubbornly reflected only her own image. 'I would have loved you forever and forever and never been unfaithful. I *do* love you. I always will. But you're dead and Bradley's alive ...'

She moaned softly, hugging her arms, holding herself as if against an inner disintegration.

'Gussie!' There was the sound of running feet on the stairs. She gazed desperately into the mirror but only the room was reflected: the room and her own anguished eyes.

'Goodbye, dear love,' she said and pressed a kiss against the cold glass.

'For goodness' sake, Gussie! Your father's on the verge of a heart attack. Here are your flowers. Aren't they beautiful?' Tina Lafayette pressed a posy of white roses and long satin streamers into her hand. 'Ready, sweetheart? This really is fun. There's even a crowd outside St Michel, waiting to wish you well. Your wedding seems to have grasped everyone's imagination.'

Gussie stood at the top of the sweeping staircase and heard a concerted gasp of admiration from the servants gathered in the hall. She took a deep breath. One part of her life was over and another about to begin. She was committing herself to Bradley and Beau had freed her. She had wanted his blessing: wanted him to tell her that now he, too, would be at peace. He had not done so. His presence had simply drifted away ...

Bradley. She must think of Bradley.

'I've never seen you more beautiful, Augusta,' her father said sincerely as she took his arm.

She smiled up at him, happy that he was happy.

Mae adjusted the wedding veil and Tina dabbed in the vicinity of her eyes, careful not to touch them and ruin her make-up, as Charles Lafayette led his daughter to the waiting limousine.

Gussie waved to the small group of spectators at St Michel's gates, her smile spontaneous. Eden relaxed. Gussie's odd mood had been dispelled. She was looking as radiant as any bride. The sky was cloudless; the sun brilliant. It was going to be a perfect day.

From inside the cathedral came the strains of 'Prière a Notre Dame'.

'Seven minutes late,' Tina Lafayette said with satisfaction as they were greeted in the porch by a smiling priest. 'Just long enough to make Bradley edgy.'

'Ready, Augusta?' her father asked tenderly.

Her eyes sparkled behind her veil. 'Yes, Daddy. Let's go.'

Mendelsshon's 'Wedding March' rang out. The packed congregation rose to its feet, necks craning for a first glimpse of the bride. Eden's eyes wandered to the cathedral windows. The sun had vanished, and storm clouds were brewing. They blew up more suddenly and violently in New Orleans than in any other place she knew. She frowned. A torrential downpour was the last thing they needed as they left the cathedral. It would mean a hasty dash to the cars and a dramatic curtailing of photographs.

Gussie's eyes were fixed firmly on the back of Bradley's head. She felt suffused with an almost unbearable sense of love and tenderness. His dark hair curled indecently low in a manner she knew her father would disapprove of if the young man had been any other than Bradley. Jason Shreve stood at his side, his neck flushed. Gussie's mouth curved in a smile. She could imagine Jason's discomfort at taking part in a ceremony before the town's leading citizens.

In the distance, surmounting the rich, stately strains of the 'Wedding March', there came the low rumble of thunder. Gussie was unperturbed. It had thundered that day in

115

Jackson Square when Bradley had seized her and kissed her for the first time. It was romantic that thunder should return on her wedding day, reminding her of that occasion: of the moment when she had first been aware of the intensity of Bradley's feelings for her.

Her gaze flicked away from Bradley's waiting figure and over the heads of the congregation. She could see Desirée in a lime-green dress and matching pill-box hat, looking unexpectedly sophisticated. Shreves, Ashingtons, Jeffersons, Alexanders, Delatours, Lafittes, Hamptons, Merriweathers, Villères, Labarres, Brennans and Fairmonts abounded. No one had been forgotten. No one omitted from the invitation list. Bradley had seen to that. He'd wanted his schoolfriends and colleagues at his wedding, and Charles Lafayette had had to capitulate.

The priest stepped forward. Gussie was at Bradley's side. She turned and handed her bouquet to Mae and then looked towards Bradley, suddenly shy. He grinned, his dark eyes reassuring as the priest who had known them since childhood greeted the congregation.

Normally Father Keane was not in favour of early marriages, but in this case he felt no doubt as to the young people's future happiness. Bradley Hampton was a fine young man, mature beyond his years. He smiled down at them as the guests began to sing 'Love Divine, All Love Excelling'.

The cathedral darkened and Mrs Jefferson gazed up from her hymn book nervously. She was afraid of thunder and the approaching storm promised to be severe.

'In the name of the Father, and of the Son, and of the Holy Spirit . . .' Father Keane's voice was deep, resonant.

'Amen.'

Thunder rolled in the distance.

116

'The grace of our Lord Jesus Christ and the love of God and the fellowship of the Holy Spirit be with you all.'

'And also with you.'

Gussie's lips were suddenly dry as the hundreds of voices behind her filled the beautiful building. The wave of joy that had supported her as she walked down the aisle was fast ebbing and she sought vainly to keep a hold on it.

Father Keane was now reading Gussie's favourite passage from the New Testament. She tried to concentrate on the words but her mind was tugging to be free.

'This is the word of the Lord,' Father Keane concluded. 'Thanks be to God.'

Gussie's lips moved but no sound came from them. She heard Bradley at her side: firm, assured, confident. Bradley. She must think of Bradley. She must not let Beau intrude on the most private part of her relationship with Bradley.

The Responsorial Psalm was sung. A flash of lightning made several heads turn in the direction of the windows. Gussie kept her eyes firmly on the high altar. Bradley. She was marrying Bradley. This was her wedding service. Soon they would be exchanging their wedding vows. Soon they would be man and wife. Beau's face swam before her, dark, lean, mocking.

'Augusta and Bradley. You have come together in this church so that the Lord may seal and strengthen your love in the presence of the church's minister and this community.'

Gussie closed her eyes, trying to chase the image away. It remained against her pressed lids: sensually aware, sensually arousing.

'Christ abundantly blesses this love. He has already consecrated you in baptism and now he enriches and strengthens you by special sacrament so that you may assume the duties of marriage in mutual and lasting fidelity.'

Gussie felt a bead of sweat break out on her forehead as she opened her eyes once more.

'Please go away,' she whispered silently. 'Please! *Please!*'

'And so, in the presence of the church, I ask you to state your intentions.'

Father Keane's eyes were drawn momentarily to the soaring windows. The October sky was as black as night, the rolls of thunder following one upon the other in rapid succession. He returned his attention to the young couple before him.

'Augusta and Bradley. I shall now ask you to freely undertake the obligations of marriage, and to state that there is no legal impediment to your marriage. Are you ready to do this, and without reservation, to give yourselves to each other in marriage?'

'I am.' Bradley's deep-timbred voice was audible even to those at the rear of the cathedral.

Augusta tried to speak and failed. Father Keane smiled at her encouragingly. The most spirited of girls were often overcome by the ceremony of their own marriage.

'I ...' Beau's face swam before her, the black glittering eyes challenging her. Daring her.

'I am,' said a voice that could not possibly be hers.

'Are you ready to love and honour each other as man and wife for the rest of your lives?'

The harsh lines of Beau's mouth were savage.

'I am,' Bradley said without the least hesitation.

The congregation waited for the bride's response. Feet shifted. The centre of the storm was fast approaching, brilliant flashes of lightning rending the darkened sky.

Gussie closed her eyes. Her father's pride turned to concern.

'I am,' Gussie whispered, so low that only Father Keane heard her.

Thunder drowned his next words. He waited a few seconds and then continued, raising his voice to combat the disruptive elements.

'Are you ready to accept children lovingly from God, and bring them up according to the law of Christ and his church?'

'I am.' If Bradley was aware of Gussie's inner turmoil, he showed no sign of it. With glazed eyes Gussie looked at Father Keane and towards the high altar. Beau had gone.

She could see flowers and altar boys and Father Keane's face, prompting and concerned. What had he just said? What did she have to respond?

'I am,' she said, her voice tremulous.

Father Keane was looking at Bradley. 'Please say after me, "I do solemnly declare ..."'

'I do solemnly declare ...'

Beau's face no longer hovered before her but he was there. She could feel his anger; his rage; his passionate jealousy.

'... why I, Bradley Hampton, should not be joined in matrimony to Augusta Lafayette.'

Candles flickered. The gloom of the cathedral was oppressive. Small hands slipped into strong ones as lightning ripped the sky. The congregation was accustomed to sudden, violent storms, but this was the worst anyone could remember.

She had to speak. She had to make her responses. The thunder and the lightning were no longer nostalgic reminders of her first encounter with Bradley. They were terrifying reminders of the storm that had accompanied the burial of Laetitia Clay. Reminders that Beau's body had been seized from its resting place.

'After me, Augusta, please,' Father Keane was saying.

She felt enveloped in darkness. Father Keane's face swam disorientatedly before her.

119

'I do solemnly declare . . .'

The skin of her hands and arms tingled. The nape of her neck felt cold. Her spine chilled.

'. . . that I know not . . .'

She couldn't be sick on her wedding day: not before the whole of New Orleans and in the gown of French lace her grandmother and mother had worn before her.

'. . . of any lawful impediment . . . why I . . . Augusta Lafayette . . .'

She was swamped by heat, drowning in sweat.

'. . . may not be joined in matrimony to Bradley Hampton.'

'Augusta! Augusta!'

It came so loud and clear that she gasped and nearly fell.

Mae stood horrified. Eden stepped forward hastily, catching Gussie's arm and steadying her.

Gussie gazed round her, wild-eyed. Hadn't Bradley and Father Keane heard? Why were they looking at her like that?

Father Keane was saying, 'Since it is your intention to enter into marriage, declare your consent before God and his church.'

'Never, Augusta! Never! You are mine! Mine forever. Forever . . .'

Gussie cried out, her arms reaching as if to grasp something that was not there.

'Would you like me to halt the service?' Father Keane asked Bradley in a low voice.

'No.' Bradley gave Charles Lafayette no chance to express an opinion.

Rain lashed the windows. The very sky seemed to be falling in around them.

'Very well.' Father Keane took another anxious look at the bride and said to Bradley, 'Bradley Hampton, will you take

Augusta Lafayette, here present, for your lawful wife, according to the rite of our Holy Mother, the Church?'

'I will.'

There was a noise in her ears like a thousand waves.

'Augusta Lafayette, will you take Bradley Hampton, here present, for your lawful husband, according to the rite of our Holy Mother, the Church?'

'*AUGUSTA!*' It was a shout of rage.

With a low moan she swung on her heel, away from the altar, away from Father Keane. The cathedral doors crashed open and lightning knifed down the aisle.

Mrs Jefferson threw herself on her knees, convinced that her last moment had come. There were screams and cries of panic. Bradley's arm shot out to restrain Gussie but she had no need of restraint. Her headlong flight was halted. *He* was there. There, for everyone to see. Dark and terrible in his rage, silhouetted against the flaring sky.

'*Beau!*' She wrenched herself away from Bradley's grasp and with a broken sob began to run, run, to where he was waiting for her.

The lightning flashed again, blinding in its intensity. She was caught in its jagged path, caught and pinned, falling senselessly to the blood-red carpet, her white skirts billowing around her.

To Eden's petrified gaze she looked like a small, defence-less, murdered dove. It seemed an eternity before anyone could break the stupor of shock and run to her aid. Bradley was the first to regain control of his senses. Grim-faced he ran down the aisle between the pews of stunned and terrified guests and seized his bride. His bride, but not his wife. Father Keane was at his side. Jason Shreve was desperately clearing a way through hysterical relatives to the vestry.

'Who *was* that guy?' Mr Jefferson asked wildly as people pushed past him, struggling to get a better view.

'Who in his right mind would crash into a wedding ceremony like that?' Shenton Ross Sr said, unable to answer him.

'Seeking shelter, I guess,' a Lafayette relation said, wiping perspiration from his brow and striving to maintain an appearance of calm.

'Shelter? He wasn't even wet!'

The clamour of voices was deafening. Reverence had been replaced by pandemonium.

'Dear God, but I thought the Devil himself had entered,' Mrs Ashington said tremulously, supported by her husband.

'Where did he go?' Hamptons and Lafayettes asked in unison.

'Why did Gussie run?' Natalie Jefferson asked, clutching at the pew for support.

'Scared out of her wits, poor child,' the woman next to her said.

'Some hell of an entrance. Who *was* he?' Mr Jefferson demanded again as elegant hatted women pushed past him, eager to reach open air.

'It looked like . . .' a stunned Mr Alexander began.

'For Christ's sake! Don't say that! There are enough wild rumours already!' Mr Jefferson mopped his brow again and stumbled into the aisle.

Leaving Augusta temporarily in the care of her fiancé and parent, Father Keane returned to calm the near-hysterical congregation.

'Dear Brethren. On behalf of Mr Charles Lafayette, I am requested to inform you that because of his daughter's health, the wedding will not take place as planned. At least, not today. The reception will be as arranged and he will meet with you all at St Michel. Thank you.'

The buzz of speculation increased. What did Father

122

Keane mean? 'Due to Gussie's health?' What was wrong with Gussie's health? Now that the centre of the storm had passed, courage was returning to shattered nerves. *They* were feeling all right now. A little shaky, as anyone might be after nearly being struck by lightning, but all right, just the same. Surely, in a few moments, Augusta could have returned to her place at Bradley's side?

'Did you hear what she called? I swear to you it was Beau. Beau Clay. I know the thunder was deafening, but I'd stake my life on it,' a Hampton relative said authoritatively.

'Bradley. She was calling for Bradley. The lightening terrified her,' the woman at his side corrected.

'And she looked so beautiful coming down the aisle. Happy and radiant,' Natalie Jefferson said, dabbing at her eyes with a handkerchief that matched her dress. 'That storm's ruined everything.'

'Never mind. There's still the reception. Charles Lafayette never stints on the quality of his caviar and champagne,' Mrs Ashington said, patting Mrs Jefferson's hand and smiling vacantly at someone across the aisle.

Noisily they made their exit from the cathedral they had entered so respectfully a short while before. Eden and Mae were ushered quickly into a Lafayette limousine. Only Judge Clay remained seated, half-turned as everyone else had been when the doors had crashed open and the intruder entered, shattering the last shreds of Gussie's nerves. A galaxy of flowered hats now bobbed beneath the porch, scurrying for cars and chauffeurs and the anticipation of more gossip at St Michel. Judge Clay remained immobile: staring into space in stunned disbelief.

'Augusta, Jim Meredith is here ...' Her father's anxious voice permeated her consciousness.

'Gussie! Gussie! Can you hear me?'

It was strange to hear such naked emotion in Bradley's voice: a tone almost of fear. She opened her eyes, her fingers tightening imperceptibly in his grasp. Bradley's arms were around her, her head was resting against his chest.

'Thank God!' her father said, mopping his face with a large silk handkerchief. 'Now perhaps you will believe there's something wrong with my daughter, Jim. Three times! Three times she's collapsed like this and you keep telling me it's nothing to worry about! I want the best, Jim. Tests, checks, everything.'

'Let me carry you, Gussie.' Bradley's face, so joyful only moments before, was ravaged.

'No!'

Charles Lafayette turned his attention back to his daughter and prospective son-in-law. 'No. We're not leaving here until Augusta can walk. To be seen being carried will only intensify the gossip. That lightning was the worst I've ever experienced. There wasn't a woman in the place who wasn't terrified out of her skin. And then that maniac . . .' He broke off. He didn't want to dwell on thoughts of the dark, powerful figure whose entrance had been almost a physical blow. 'They'll understand her fainting . . .'

'Don't get upset, Daddy,' she said quietly. 'I can walk. Let's go home.'

Tenderly Bradley raised her to her feet and circled her waist with his arm.

'I've had to let the reception go on as planned,' Charles Lafayette said to no one in particular. His composure had completely deserted him. 'What do we do now? Continue the ceremony at the house while the guests are assembled? Yes, yes. I think that would be best.' He paced the room nervously. 'The main salon will hold all the Lafayettes and Hamptons . . .'

'No.' Three heads turned to Gussie in varying degrees of

surprise. 'No. I don't want to continue the wedding ceremony at St Michel.'

'But it would make life easier, Augusta,' her father said, a desperate edge to his voice.

'No.' She was so pale that her skin seemed almost translucent. 'You don't understand. There isn't going to be another wedding ceremony.'

'But of course there is . . .' her father began.

'What do you mean, Gussie?' Bradley's voice was urgent. He halted, still supporting her, and stared down at her vacant expression. .

'I'm not going to marry you, Bradley,' she said unsteadily. 'I can't.'

'What do you mean, can't?' her father ranted, shrugging off Father Keane's restraining arm. 'Are we to look complete fools? This is your wedding day, Augusta! I've planned it for months! A small simple ceremony in the main salon . . .'

'No.' Bradley silenced him, his eyes full of anguish. 'No. If Gussie has no wish to continue the ceremony today, then we'll postpone it.'

'But the guests . . .' Charles Lafayette protested.

'Damn the guests!' Bradley said and, ignoring Charles Lafayette's former pleas, he swung Augusta up into his arms and carried her out into the weak sunlight that was filtering through the receding clouds.

Gussie didn't speak again as Bradley drove her home in a Hampton limousine. Silently she allowed him to carry her up one of St Michel's rear flights of stairs, avoiding the guests, and lay her on her bed. For a long moment he stood by her side, holding her hand, and then said gently, 'Sleep, sweetheart. I'll see you tomorrow. We'll talk then.'

Only her eyes answered him. Filled with such unspeakable sadness that the breath caught in his throat. Blindly he stumbled from the room, ran down the staircase, pushed past startled guests and leaped into his car. Charles Lafayette could go on with his mockery of a reception but he was having no part of it. He had lost Gussie and he did not know why.

Gussie lay very still. From downstairs came the sounds of voices and laughter and champagne corks. Festivities for a non-existent bride. They would never understand: not her father, not Bradley. She couldn't tell them. She would have to live with the secret lifelong, with the result of a silly, girlish prank. The sadness in her eyes turned to suffering. Because of it, Beau had died and had found no peace. Her obsessive love for him had led to his eternal torment.

Silent tears stole down her cheeks. Forever. She had never realized what forever meant. Never comprehended the magnitude of it. She would have to live out the whole of her life alone. Watching as Bradley gradually withdrew from her, finding tenderness elsewhere: love. Being a guest at his wedding instead of his bride. Her heart hurt with the pain of it. She would become like Mae's grandmother. An oddity to be pointed out and whispered about: all because she had sat before her mirror and willed with all her heart and soul for Beauregard Clay's unending devotion.

CHAPTER SIX

Jim Meredith had come to give her a sedative. Her father had come in several times and had stood at the foot of her bed, gazing with increasing concern at her glazed eyes. Tina Lafayette had held her hand and talked softly and comfortingly but had received no replies. Augusta had sunk into a world of silence, consumed by her own thoughts, oblivious of those around her. When the bride-to-be had failed to put in an appearance at the lavish reception, Charles Lafayette had announced smoothly, but sadly, that Dr Meredith was attending her and that she was suffering from a fierce flu virus and would be incapacitated for several days: possibly two weeks or maybe three.

'I'm sorry, Bradley. She's not well enough to see anyone,' Charles Lafayette had said awkwardly when Bradley had arrived the next morning.

Bradley had stared at him, his jaw muscles tensing. For once he had not argued with his future father-in-law. He had simply swung on his heel and strode towards his car, intent, apparently, on speaking with Dr Meredith and discovering the true situation for himself.

Charles Lafayette breathed a sigh of relief, remembering those agonizing moments. He had no desire for Bradley to see Augusta in her present condition. If Bradley saw her, he might think twice about going ahead with the wedding. Augusta's passivity was far more disquieting than hysteria would have been.

He paced his study restlessly. When she had fainted on her

birthday she had recovered within minutes: bouncy and vivacious as ever. When she had fainted at Laetitia Clay's funeral she had taken longer to return to her normal self, but she had done so – eventually. This time he was filled with grim foreboding. It was as if his Augusta, the little girl he loved so deeply, had slipped away from him and left a stranger in her place. A stranger whose mind was closed to him. Even Jim Meredith had been disconcerted and had promised to contact a psychiatrist friend of his. A man who was a specialist in cases of emotional disturbance. He slammed his fist hard on his desk. Damn it. She couldn't be like her grandmother. She *couldn't*.

Besides, his mother's death had been an accident. Not suicide. He had never believed what the gossips had believed: what the family had believed. His mother had been young; happy; in love. Why should she have waded deep into the stagnant waters of the bayous and extinguished her own life? It was a question he had asked himself a hundred times.

Doubt, insidious and never quite stilled, gripped him. Perhaps his mother *had* been sick. There had been other rumours down the years. Rumours about Leila Jefferson. And Leila and his mother had been inseparable.

He clenched his fists. There was nothing wrong with Augusta. Nothing abnormal about *his* little girl. Why, then, was she behaving so strangely? Goddammit. She had *wanted* to marry Bradley. She had everything a girl could desire. What, in heaven's name, was the matter with her?

At the time, Charles had thought that what he had told the guests at the reception would give plenty of leeway for Augusta's recovery. Now he was not so sure. Two weeks had already passed and Augusta was no nearer to being her laughing, vivacious self than she had been when she had regained consciousness in the vestry. It was as if an inner light had been quenched. She no longer glowed with life and health and vitality. She remained in her room, sitting for long, silent hours at her dressing table, gazing into the oval mirror as if therein lay the answer to her misery. Jim Meredith had come again, Dr Wallace, a young, slick-suited New Yorker in his wake. Charles had regarded the man distrustfully, but Jim Meredith had promised that no one would know that they had resorted to psychiatry. Not even Bradley.

Since then the unnervingly young Dr Wallace had moved into St Michel, and now spent the greater part of each day with Gussie. Apart from Charles and Jim Meredith, only Tina Lafayette knew of his presence. Fortunately, Bradley, respecting Jim Meredith's judgment, had promised not to force his presence on Augusta until she was willing, of her own accord, to see him. He had anticipated a wait of days – not weeks. He had visited the house two, three times a day and every time he left his sense of disquiet grew. Something terrible had happened to Gussie and no one would tell him what it was.

Dr Wallace emerged from Gussie's room and gravely told Jim Meredith that in his opinion Augusta Lafayette had a deep-seated father fixation: that her emotional trauma was caused by her fear of losing her father's love once she became a wife as well as a daughter.

Jim Meredith frowned and kept his thoughts to himself. In his opinion the answer was not so simple, but Wallace was the expert. He himself was only a family practitioner, accustomed to healing day-to-day infirmities – not delving into the recesses of sick minds. Nevertheless, he went to sit with Augusta himself.

'How are you feeling this morning. Augusta?'

She was sitting at her dressing table, a satin, long-sleeved robe over her négligé. At his query she turned her head away and stared through the open window and out over the lawns and trees of St Michel.

'Bradley was here about an hour ago. He's coming back this afternoon. He wants to see you very badly, Augusta.'

There was no reply.

'It's been three weeks, Augusta,' he said carefully, convinced that she had no concept of how time had passed since she had collapsed. 'Leo has returned to Vancouver. Great Aunt Belle has finally returned home, much to your father's relief. Bradley has come every day, several times a day, to see you. Your father is refusing him permission until he feels you are regaining your strength and expressing a desire to see him yourself. How about it, Augusta? He's a fine young man.'

He waited. It was as if she had not heard him. Then she turned her head slowly and his heart twisted at the pain in her violet-dark eyes.

'I don't want to see Bradley, Dr Meredith. I don't want to hurt him any further.' Her voice was low, drained of feeling. The voice of someone for whom there is no option.

Jim Meredith leaned forward and took her unprotesting hands in his.

'Why, Augusta? Why?'

'Because I can't marry him,' she said, as simply as if she were talking to a child. 'I can never marry him.'

'Don't you love him?' He tried to keep the eagerness from his voice. This was the first time she had spoken at any length since her collapse. Perhaps at last he would know the truth.

A shadow of a smile hovered at the corners of her mouth and vanished, leaving an expression of unspeakable sadness.

'Yes. I love him. But I can't marry him. Not ever.'

'But *why*?' Jim Meredith's voice throbbed with urgency. Was Dr Wallace correct? *Did* Augusta have a father fixation that they were unaware of?

She turned away from him, staring sightlessly into the dressing-table mirror.

'I gave my word to someone else,' she said, and large tears glittered in the depths of her eyes. 'I can never be free of that vow. Never.'

Jim Meredith felt relief swamp him. So much for psychiatry. Augusta had been unfaithful to Bradley and was now consumed with regret and guilt.

'Only a wedding vow is binding,' he said compassionately. 'No other vow can hold you.'

A smile, wordly-wise, strangely knowing on so young a face, tinged her lips. 'The vow I took has bound me more firmly than any wedding vow, Dr Meredith. Wedding vows are only until death.'

'I don't understand you, Augusta. What vow did you make?'

She tilted her head slightly on one side, her hair skimming her waist, her eyes suddenly puzzled.

'I didn't promise anything . . .'

'Then what did you say?'

'Nothing.' Staring into the glass she began to laugh softly, mirthlessly. 'Nothing at all. I just *willed* him and now he won't let me be free. Not ever.'

Filled with disquiet, Jim Meredith rose to his feet and stood behind her, resting his hands on her shoulders.

'*Who* did you will, Augusta? Who is it you believe has a hold over you?'

Her disconcerting laughter ceased. Through the glass her eyes met his. Intelligent and sane, deadly sure.

'Beauregard Clay,' she said and began to weep.

★

131

Dr Wallace did not accept Dr Meredith's opinion that Augusta's distress was caused by her infatuation with the dead Beau Clay. Father and daughter had lived together at St Michel for fifteen years. The result was a relationship with incestuous overtones.

Jim Meredith called him a fool and told Charles that he had made a mistake in asking for Dr Wallace's opinion. Charles Lafayette paid Dr Wallace lavishly and saw him off the premises within the hour.

Jim Meredith nursed a brandy and thought hard. It would serve no good purpose to tell Charles what Augusta had told him. Charles would find such a reason for his daughter's behaviour totally unacceptable and would probably not even believe it. It was a confidence he must keep: for the time being. He would treat Augusta himself; visit her daily; gain her trust. Time. With time, everything would be resolved.

Bradley Hampton had run out of time.

'I'm sorry, sir,' he stormed at Charles Lafayette. 'But I'm going to see Gussie.'

Charles Lafayette protested in vain. Jim Meredith laid a restraining hand on his arm and said quietly

'I think Bradley *should* see Augusta.'

Reluctantly Charles Lafayette stood by as Bradley strode towards the staircase, taking the crimson-carpeted stairs two at a time.

'He won't marry her now, Jim. A Hampton and a Lafayette. It would have been such a good marriage.'

'It still may be, Charles. He loves her and she loves him.'

'Then what in hell's name is wrong?' Charles asked tormentedly. 'What has happened to Augusta?'

Jim Meredith didn't answer him because he didn't know. Or at least not enough. He intended speaking to the

Alexanders' daughter. She was a level-headed girl and close to Augusta. She had been bridesmaid at the hastily terminated wedding ceremony. He would ask her why Augusta should feel bound to a man dead for many months and who, to his knowledge, had never paid her the slightest attention.

'Gussie! I was beginning to think you were dead and they were scared to tell me.' Bradley crossed the room in swift strides and folded her in his arms. She trembled, but no arms circled his neck and when he tried to kiss her she averted her head.

'What's the matter, Gussie? There's nothing so bad you can't tell me.'

She tried to move away from him but he refused to let her go.

'Gussie!' His voice was naked with desire and love. 'What is it that troubles you? Please tell me.'

'I can't.' Sobs rose in her throat.

His hold tightened. 'It doesn't matter what you've done. It won't alter the way I love you. Do you understand that, Gussie?' He hooked a finger under her chin and stared challengingly down at her. 'I love you, Gussie. Nothing you can say or do will alter that.'

She gave a little sound full of pain and anguish.

'I want to marry you and take you away from New Orleans. At least for a little while. We could go to Europe. Anywhere. Father Keane will marry us right here, at St Michel, this afternoon. Your father and Dr Meredith will serve as witnesses.'

'No!' She twisted free of his hold. 'No! I can't marry you, Bradley. Not ever!'

'*Why?*' His eyes were frenzied.

She was gasping for breath, the blood beating wildly in her ears. 'Because I don't love you!' she lied.

The silence was terrible. It yawned between them like a chasm that could not be bridged. His eyes held hers, unbelieving at first, then masked with pain. Very slowly he turned on his heel and left the room, the door swinging open behind him.

She swayed on her feet, the back of her hand pressed to her mouth. He was going. He would never come to St Michel again. Never hold her; never tease her; never love her. With a cry of anguish she ran to the door and the landing beyond. He was in the hall, striding, unspeaking, past her father and Jim Meredith. Striding towards the door and his car.

'Bradley!' His name screamed in her head, but could find no utterance. *'Bradley!'*

The door slammed in his wake.

'Bradley!'

This time her fevered cry filled the house. Her father and Jim Meredith were racing up the stairs towards her but Bradley had gone. She had set him free. Free, as she herself would never be.

'Augusta, for God's sake.' Her father's hands seized her shoulders.

Obediently she allowed herself to be propelled into her room. Now was the waiting time. Now surely he would come to her.

There was no longer any talk of when the Hampton/ Lafayette wedding would take place. Callers, refused entry time and time again at St Michel, ceased to come. The porch swing gathered dust; the pool was covered. Mae Jefferson and Austin Merriweather married and moved to Atlanta. Augusta had been invited to the wedding, but the letter declining the invitation had been in Charles's handwriting.

Still, Beau didn't come. It was as if, sure of her fidelity, he no longer needed to remind her of his presence. Through long sleepless nights Gussie waited in vain for his voice; for his presence. Her cheeks became hollow: her eyes blue-shadowed.

Bradley Hampton took Eden Alexander out with increasing regularity, and there were rumours that a wedding was afoot, but nothing came of it, and Eden continued her relationship with Dean.

Charles Lafayette resigned his directorships and was no longer seen at civic functions. Augusta was never seen at all. Rumour had it that she had gone to London: to Paris: to Rome. No one knew, and the less they knew the more they talked.

As the months passed, gossip faded, only to be renewed when the preparations for another Mardi Gras began. After all, Augusta Lafayette had been a queen of Mardi Gras. Now she was a recluse. Seen by no one but her father and by the Lafayette servants, who steadfastly remained silent on the subject.

Eden wrote, telephoned and called in person at St Michel, all to no avail. In despair she wrote to Mae, expressing fears she dare not utter. The letter from Mae was terse. No. She did not share Eden's fears. Midsummer's Eve had been a prank. She was surprised that Eden even remembered it.

Eden screwed up the letter and threw it away. She knew that Mae was lying, and at last decided to pay a visit to Tina Lafayette.

They sat in the grape-hung conservatory on sun-loungers and as Eden spoke Tina threaded and rethreaded the fringe on her shawl through her fingers.

'I have not visited St Michel for a long time,' she said apologetically. 'I really don't know if my cousin and Augusta

135

are in residence or if they're away. Would you like a cocktail? A Hurricane? Nicky makes very good Hurricanes.'

A devastatingly handsome young man some fifteen years Tina Lafayette's junior mixed drinks as obediently as a butler.

'Bradley is still in love with Augusta,' Eden said, silencing Tina as she began to talk about the new boutique that had opened near the square.

'Oh!' Tina Lafayette's hands fluttered nervously. 'I'd heard that ... I thought perhaps ... You and Bradley ...'

'No. He isn't a monk. He dates a lot of girls. Too many. His dates with me are different. Purely platonic. I'm his link with Augusta: or rather, he'd *like* me to be his link with Augusta. The house is closed to him now – as it is to everyone.'

'I think that's a little exaggerated, Eden.'

'When did you last see Gussie?' Eden shot at her.

'Why, I ... Actually ...' Tina Lafayette's hands tightened on her glass.

'Exactly. I bet it's so long ago you can't even remember!'

'They like their privacy. There was so much gossip ...'

'Hardly surprising under the circumstances,' Eden said grimly to Tina, and then to herself, as if Tina Lafayette wasn't there: 'What the hell am I going to do? There must be *something*. It isn't possible. It just isn't possible ...'

Tina Lafayette stared at her with frightened eyes and did not deter her as she rose to her feet, her drink untouched, leaving without even saying goodbye.

The nicest people had begun to behave strangely, Tina reflected. Judge Clay was a broken man and even to her it seemed odd that his collapse should come after the intended Hampton/Lafayette wedding, and not before. Until then he had managed to keep up an outward appearance but now he was scarcely recognizable. He shambled about the Clay mansion, murmuring his dead son's name: speaking to him as if he were in the same room. She shivered. Beau's body had never been found. Never would be found now.

Gussie, who should have been the belle of the city, was hiding away, refusing to see even the cousin of whom she had always been so fond. Charles had become a withdrawn wraith, an anguished figure who would speak to no one. This time last year, all had been happy anticipation. There had been Gussie's birthday party and their whirlwind trip to Europe for dresses. There had been the happy preparations for Gussie's wedding. Now there was nothing but vile gossip and fevered speculation.

'Another drink, Nicky, darling,' she whispered, feeling suddenly old. 'A double, please.'

Eden drove with unusual slowness away from Tina Lafayette's sprawling home. Lives were being destroyed and it seemed impossible that the cause could have been a giggling, thoughtless, girlish game. Without intending to, she drove to the old, overgrown graveyard in the French Quarter. She turned her jacket collar up, dug her hands deep in her pockets and wandered between the cold stone of ancient family mausoleums.

The single rose before the Clay tomb was fresh, the soft petals not even beginning to brown or wither. Eden knew full well whose hand had placed it there. She stood for a long time, staring at the long-stemmed rose as the breeze ruffled the lush petals. She would write to Mae again. She would not give up. Not yet.

'A heart attack,' Jim Meredith said bleakly to Tina Lafayette, who soon after disclosed to the New Orleans elite that her cousin had been ill for a long time and that Augusta had nursed him: hence, their seclusion.

No one was surprised. To a certain extent it helped to moderate the gossip. It was a reason readily believed, but not by Jim Meredith, who had signed the death certificate; and not by Mae Merriweather and Eden Alexander.

'What will I do, Jim?' Tina sobbed helplessly. 'Who will look after Augusta?'

'Augusta doesn't need any looking after,' Jim Meredith said. 'She's not mad, Tina. Not even halfway mad.'

'Then why won't she behave normally? Why does she stay there, day after day, refusing to see people?'

Jim Meredith sighed. 'I don't know, Tina. There was a time when I thought I did, but I guess I was wrong. Perhaps being a recluse is part of Augusta's nature. Perhaps she was never meant to marry.'

'Rubbish,' Tina Lafayette said, stamping a small, expensively shod foot. 'You know that isn't so, Jim Meredith. Why, you've known Augusta since she was a baby. How can you say such things?'

'Because I don't know the real answer,' Jim Meredith said bleakly.

She was dressed entirely in black, her sun-gold hair gleaming in a chignon and topped by a tiny pill-box hat and heavy veil. She looked incredibly beautiful and utterly vulnerable.

'I don't need a sedative,' Augusta said to Jim Meredith on the morning of the funeral. 'I loved him too much to want the pain of losing him eased.'

Leo Lafayette walked with her to the first of the waiting limousines, Tina Lafayette, leaning heavily on Jim Meredith's arm, following close behind. Family members who had last been at St Michel on the occasion of the intended wedding came after, descending to the cars silently and in tears. An austere man to many people, Charles Lafayette had been a long distant patriarch to scores of Lafayettes and was sincerely mourned.

When the cortège reached Providence Memorial Park, Jim Meredith gave thanks to his Maker that Charles Lafayette was not to be buried in the St Louis Cemetry. Judge Clay, physically helped in and out of the Clay limousine by his remaining son, had insisted on attending the funeral. For his sake, if for no other, Jim was glad that the Lafayette burial place was not adjoining the desecrated family tomb.

His anxiety eased even more as the service progressed. Augusta's face streamed with silent tears but her veil shielded her from the stares of the curious. She was conducting herself with admirable dignity and Jim felt proud of her. It would give the lie to all those who whispered she had lost her mind.

Through the carefully tended woodlands of the cemetery, a blue Thunderbird approached. Jim Meredith felt a slight constriction in his chest. Bradley Hampton. He had seen Mr and Mrs Hampton among the mourners and had felt relief at Bradley's absence. He should have known that Bradley would not stay away.

Heads turned as Bradley made his way towards the large group of mourners to stand, towering and broad-shouldered, beside his parents, his burning gaze focused on where Augusta stood, her veil lifting gently in the breeze, her slender figure forlorn and alone.

Why had he come? Oh God, why? Augusta's nails dug deep into her palms. 'Because he loves you,' she told herself. 'He still loves you.' The tears that wet her cheeks were now no longer solely for her father, but also for herself. He looked so handsome; so comforting; so *safe*. If only she could throw herself into his strong arms. Have him tell her he would take care of her. Love her. If only . . .

The service was over. Leo was cutting short those who were approaching Gussie and offering her their condolences. Bradley remained where he stood, holding her with his eyes.

Gussie tried not to look in his direction. How long had it been? Three months? Six months? More? Perhaps he was married! Terrified eyes flew to his hand. Strong and olive-toned and ringless. What right did she have to be jealous? She had told him she did not love him. She had done it so that he could love elsewhere. Oh, Jesus God, why did it still hurt so much?

'This way, Augusta.' It was Leo, gentle and dependable.

'I'm sorry,' she wept as she stepped into the rear of the limousine. 'Sorry, sorry, sorry . . .'

Those who heard thought the despairing words were for her father. Jim Meredith, staring from her to the tortured figure of Bradley Hampton, knew differently. Sighing deeply, he followed Tina into her limousine. It all would have been so much easier if Gussie had been married to Bradley, and now, without Charles, Gussie would be more cut off than ever. There would be money in plenty. In theory, the world was at Gussie's feet. He sighed again. But they had already been through all the arguments, and he knew she would fight tooth and nail rather than leave the seclusion of her home. He would call in every day. There was nothing more he could do.

She watched from her bedroom window as Jim Meredith's Continental eased its way down the oak-lined drive. In the aftermath of the funeral Augusta had been pale and silent, but nothing in her behaviour had caused speculation among her array of relatives. Now they were gone and she was alone. Alone. The word sent a cold shiver down her spine. She had never been destined to live alone. She needed to love and be

140

loved. The need for Bradley was like a physical pain. She could go to him today. Now. He wouldn't turn her away. She knew he wouldn't.

'*Augusta, Augusta.*'

She gasped and pressed her hands against her eyes to shut out the invidious whisper. It was her imagination. It had to be. Beau's voice had not tormented her for weeks, for months.

She tried to recapture the decisiveness of a minute before. She had simply to walk from the room, descend the stairs, summon the chauffeur ...

'*Augusta!*'

Again she pressed the palms of her hands against her ears, willing herself to move to the door. In ten minutes she could be at the Hampton estate. Bradley would be there. He would be tense, not knowing the purpose of her visit. She would tell him she was sorry; that she loved him and wanted to marry him; that she had told a lie because ...

'*AUGUSTA!*'

She was at the door, looking down the richly carpeted stairs that wound down to the marble-floored hall. Through the glass panels of the door she could see the blurred outline of someone waiting. Fifty yards. Only fifty yards ...

'*You're mine! Mine!*' The voice was no whisper now: it was a frenzied, jealous shout.

'*No!*' she shouted back into space. '*You're dead and I'm alive!*'

Like breaking an invisible barrier, she hurled herself from the room and grasped the gleaming rosewood banisters. '*I'm going to Bradley!*'

'*Forever*,' Beau's voice said menacingly, and his shadow fell across her, pinning her back against the banisters. '*You bound me to you forever, Augusta.*'

She could feel the weight of his body, feel his breath on

her cheek. She was being pushed backwards. The banister rail dug deep into her spine; her hands slid helplessly along the smooth wood.

'*You made me love you forever, Augusta. You can't leave me now for another man. You're mine. Mine . . .*'

'Landsakes, Miss Augusta! You're going to fall to your death,' Allie shrieked, rushing up the stairs and grabbing her. 'What you think you're doing? Leaning back over the banisters that way?'

Gussie gazed at her dazedly. They were alone. Where had Beau gone? Surely he'd been here?

'Beau,' she said, as Allie ushered her back into her bedroom. 'Beau? Where are you? Where have you gone?'

'There ain't no one here,' Allie said sternly, sitting her down on her bed, removing her shoes, swinging her legs up and under the coolness of the sheets. 'You need to sleep, Miss Augusta. That's what you need.' She drew the curtains, plunging the room into darkness. 'I don't want no more such nonsense, Miss Augusta. You've no right to scare folks so.'

The door closed. Augusta stared up at the ceiling. Where had she been going? Beau had been jealous. So jealous that he had been going to come for her. Her head throbbed. Who could Beau possibly be jealous of? She'd never loved anyone but him. Except Bradley. She tried to remember Bradley's face but could not. It was swamped by Beau's hard, glittering eyes.

'*Mine,*' he whispered in her ear. '*Forever, Augusta. Forever . . .*'

She rose at dawn and stepped like a sleep-walker into the dew-damp air. She picked a large, milk-white magnolia and then stood trancelike until the limousine slid to a halt at her side.

Augusta smiled at Horatio, the quiet, well-spoken man

who had been her father's chauffeur for twenty years, and slid into the rear of the car. Horatio nodded good morning and kept his thoughts to himself. He had hoped Mr Lafayette's death would put an end to Miss Augusta's dawn trips to the St Louis Cemetery.

Yesterday's flower lay dying on the tangled grass. She replaced it with the lush magnolia.

'Forever,' she said, shivering in the early morning air. 'Forever, Beau. Just as I promised.'

'Miss Eden for you, Miss Augusta,' Allie said as the spring sunshine warmed the day. 'She's out on the back porch. 'Shall I bring you some milkshakes?'

'Yes and tell her we're coming, Allie.'

Allie stared at her. Miss Augusta was on her own. She hurried from the room. Things had been bad before Mr Lafayette had died, but now they were a hundred times worse, Miss Augusta continually talking to herself, singing late at night and into the early hours of morning; soft, coaxing singing as if she was trying to lure someone to her room. Servants who had been with the Lafayettes for years bore it stoically but the little girl from Atlanta who had come to help in the kitchen had soon fled, saying that the mistress was spooked.

The girl had received a clip around the ears from Sabina Royal, the Lafayette cook, but silently many of the staff agreed with her. There was no pleasure left in being employed at St Michel, and Miss Augusta certainly didn't behave as if she was right in her head. When Horatio had at last told them where Miss Augusta insisted on being taken every morning, the unease had deepened. The Lafayette family mausoleum was not in St Louis Cemetery. Augusta had no reason to go visiting there. Not unless . . .

Allie had told them not to be fools. Of course Miss Augusta

wasn't spooked. She was just disturbed. She would be all right again: eventually.

'Hi,' Eden said, disguising her dismay at the sight of Gussie's hollow cheeks and shadowed eyes. 'How's things?'

'Fine.' Gussie sat next to Eden on the faded cushions of the porch swing as Allie came out with the drinks. Eden felt a surge of relief. This was more like old times. At least Gussie had not refused to see her.

'How are you finding it? Living here by yourself?' Eden asked when Allie had gone.

'Oh, I'm not by myself,' Gussie said composedly.

'Is Tina staying with you?'

'No.'

'Then who is?'

'Beau Clay,' Gussie said, swinging rhythmically. 'I told you he was here last time you came but you didn't believe me.'

Eden stared at her with horrified eyes. 'Beau Clay is dead, Gussie.'

'I know. You said that before, too. He's dead, but his being dead doesn't make any difference – not to Beau. I've bound him to me forever.' She leaned towards Eden, her eyes feverish. 'And he's going to come for me, Eden. Soon. Today, Tomorrow. *Soon!*'

Eden felt as if she would never breathe again. 'Bradley,' she croaked at last, 'what about Bradley? He still loves you, Gussie.'

Desolation swept Gussie's face. 'Does he?'

For a hair's-breadth of time Eden thought she had broken the sickness of Gussie's mind and then Gussie said sadly, 'But I promised Beau first. I told him I would love him and want him forever. Vows have to be kept, Eden. Bradley said so.'

'I'm going to see Mae's grandmother,' Eden said shakily,

rising to her feet. 'She started all this, she'll know what to do.'

'It's too late, Eden,' Gussie said, her eyes brilliant with fear. 'Beau won't wait any longer for me. He's going to come for me! I know he is!'

'Jesus and Mary,' Eden whispered. 'You've got to do something, Gussie. Quickly!'

'Too late,' Gussie said again and leaned back against the cushions, the fire dying from her eyes. 'It's too late, Eden.'

Eden ran for her car and turned the ignition with trembling fingers. Something had to be done immediately or Gussie would be put in a State mental institution. She swerved out of the driveway, just missing an oncoming car. She had never met Leila Jefferson, though she had heard the rumours. She crashed a set of lights. But those rumours were nothing compared to those that would soon be circulating about Gussie. She skidded into the broad drive of the Jefferson home. Should she have gone for Bradley first? Told Bradley what had happened on that distant Midsummer's Eve? She slammed the car door behind her. No. Bradley was in love with Gussie. He could not be expected to accept that her mental derangement was due to an obsession with another man. Once the spectre of Beau Clay had been erased, Gussie would return to normal and her relationship with Bradley would take care of itself.

'You want to see my mother-in-law, Eden?' Mrs Jefferson asked incredulously. 'I'm afraid I don't understand.'

Eden forced a brilliant smile. 'I'm doing some research on Old New Orleans and I thought Mrs Jefferson Sr could help me out. Mae said she knew a hundred and one stories about the beginning of the city.'

'Yes.' Mae's mother was unenthusiastic. She knew some of the stories her mother-in-law told and didn't approve of them. 'I'm sure she would have loved to have helped you,

145

Eden, but I'm afraid she isn't here. She doesn't live with us: not that we haven't asked her, of course – '

'Oh, that doesn't matter, I'd love to go see her. Only I don't know where the old Jefferson place is . . .' she said disarmingly.

Mrs Jefferson had no intention of telling her. It was a decrepit, near-derelict place and a disgrace to the family. The thought of anyone visiting there gave her vapours.

'I'm afraid I can't help you, Eden,' she said firmly. 'My mother-in-law receives no visitors. It's been very nice seeing you but now I must ask you to excuse me. The secretary of the Rose Club has just called and . . .'

Eden made a speedy exit. There was no point in staying. She drove to the nearest diner and ordered a hamburger and coke. Then she phoned Desirée.

'The Jefferson place? Why do you want to know?' The edge of permanent hysteria in Desirée's voice heightened.

'To hell with why I want to know,' Eden snapped 'Where is it?'

'Down near the Gulf; deep in the bayous.'

'But *where?*' Eden demanded, wishing she could shake Desirée by her silly shoulders.

'I don't *know* where!' Desirée said, her voice rising alarmingly. 'What ever do you – '

Eden slammed the phone down. She ate her hamburger without tasting it and then rang the Shreve house, the Ross's house, the Lafittes and the Delatours. No one could give an accurate address for the old Jefferson plantation. No one but the Jeffersons had ever been there. Eden swore under her breath and rang Mae in Atlanta.

'But why?' Mae asked nervously.

'Because Gussie is losing her mind,' Eden yelled brutally. 'The only person capable of breaking her delusion is your grandmother.'

146

There was a long silence and the Mae said tremulously, 'What if it isn't a delusion, Eden?'

Eden's voice lost its usual authoritativeness. 'Of course it's a delusion.'

'*I* don't believe it's a delusion,' Mae sobbed. 'I believe it's the truth,' and she slammed the phone down, and no matter how many times Eden rang again, refused to answer it.

Eden crossed the Mississippi on the Greater New Orleans Bridge and headed west. Mae had said that the original Jefferson home was near Sulphur amongst the swamplands in the vicinity of Calcasieu Lake. Once in the area she would be able to find someone to direct her. Paying little heed to the speed limit she pressed her foot down hard on the accelerator and sped along the West Bank Expressway, her brow furrowed.

'You see, my love, I told her,' Gussie said, pushing the swing into motion with her foot, oblivious of the afternoon's passing. 'Why do you tease me? Why do you make me afraid?'

Allie put the empty milkshake glasses on a tray, saying unsteadily, 'Who are you talking to, Miss Augusta? There ain't nobody there.'

'Beau is here,' Gussie said, twisting a long strand of golden hair around her finger.

The glasses rattled on the tray. 'Beau who, Miss Augusta?'

'Beau Clay,' Augusta said. 'He's always here. He likes it here, Allie. He likes the garden and the trees. He likes to stand beneath the branches and watch.' Her eyes darkened introspectively. 'Soon he will come inside, Allie. Soon he will not be content to stay in the garden. He will come inside and take me away.'

'Lordy, Lordy, it's time someone took *her* away,' Sabina

said, removing her apron, the fat on her upper arms quivering. 'I ain't staying here another day. That girl ain't right in the head and there ain't no one can tell me that she is.' She rammed a hat on to her head. 'Heaven help her, that's all I say.'

'Are you going as well?' Allie asked fearfully as Louis entered the kitchen, his jacket and waistcoat replaced by a sweater, a suitcase in his hand.

'I'm afraid so. She talked to him all through lunch, just as if he were there. I can't take that. No matter how good the wages.'

'But there's going to be nobody left,' Allie wailed.

'There's Horatio,' Sabina said, throwing her belongings into a basket, '. . . and there's Beau Clay!'

Allie shrieked and buried her head in her hands, sobbing convulsively. 'Miss Augusta won't mind if you leave,' Louis said kindly, 'She won't even notice, Allie.'

Allie raised a tear-stained face. 'I can't leave her. Not now. She's ill.'

'She's spooked,' Sabina said. 'If you'd a mite of sense you'd get yourself out of here – right now.'

Allie shook her head dumbly. She would stay. Horatio would look after her.

Gussie was uninterested in the exodus of St Michel's staff when Allie told her. She didn't want to eat anyway. Dusk fell and a breeze stirred the leaves of the trees, lifting the lightness of the mosquito netting that hung against the side of the window as she sat before her mirror, brushing her hair and staring into the glass, willing him to appear.

'Will it be soon, my love?' she asked. 'Will it be tonight?'

She was wearing the white silk dress her father had been

so fond of. It was simple and unsophisticated. Not the sort of dress she would have worn to go out with Beau.

She crossed to the wardrobe and opened the door, running her hand along racks of dresses.

'Which dress should I wear?'

Her hand was invisibly stilled. Beneath her fingers was the rose-pink gown she had worn on the night of his death. A little sigh escaped from her lips. Tonight she would be ready for him. Tonight she would have a lover. Tonight she would be normal again.

With great care she bathed and perfumed her body and stepped into the softness of the ankle-length gown. The colour warmed and flattered her cheeks. She set the lamp near the window and opened her bedroom door. Then she sat on the dressing table stool and waited, eyes closed, hands folded in her lap like an innocent Madonna.

Allie approached the room nervously, the glass of warm milk she carried rattling on the small tray. Miss Augusta's aunt had instructed that she was to make sure Miss Augusta drank her milk and took her sleeping tablets every night. The door was ajar. There was a stillness about the house that was unnerving.

'Miss Augusta? Are you all right?'

Hesitantly Allie entered the room.

'*Augusta!*' The voice sighed past her, filling the room. '*Augusta! Augusta!*'

The milk and the tray crashed to the floor. Augusta leapt to her feet and imprisoned the fleeing Allie by the wrists.

'No! Allie, wait! Watch! He's coming! Don't drive him away!'

Sheer terror rooted Allie to the spot. The room was silent again. From outside came the sound of the night wind

149

soughing through the tops of the trees and then, unmistakeably, there came the faint sound of footsteps on the gravel of the drive.

Allie stifled a scream as Augusta's finger dug deep into her flesh. 'Did you hear that, Allie? He's coming for me! It's nearly over!'

'Holy Mary,' Allie moaned, her face ashen.

'He's there! I know he's there!' Gussie turned to the open door, her eyes wild.

Eden roared down the avenue, the tyres screaming as she entered St Michel's drive. It was nearly midnight and she had accomplished nothing. Everyone in Sulphur knew of Leila Jefferson. Everyone had heard of the Jefferson place, but no one could tell her how to get there. And without directions it would be difficult to explore the forest and marshlands in safety. Eden would drive to Atlanta and force Mae to return with her. They would see her grandmother together. The drive curved, the oaks thinned. At Gussie's window a lamp burned, but the rest of the house was dark and silent, strangely forbidding. Her headlights flicked past the last of the trees and illuminated the porticoed entrance. A dark figure stood between the fluted pillars, his hand on the great, brass Georgian door-knocker.

The car swerved and bumped wildly on to grass. Bradley. What was Bradley doing at St Michel at near midnight and where was his car?

By the time she had regained control of the Cadillac, the doors of St Michel were wide open and a fleeing figure was hurling itself down the shallow stairs and towards her. She ran from the car.

'What's is it? What's the matter, Allie?'

'It's Miss Augusta! She's plum out of her mind!'

Eden seized the hysterical maid, shaking her violently. 'What's happened, Allie? Is Augusta safe?'

'He was coming for her, Miss Eden! I heard him myself! I heard his voice in the room and then I heard his footsteps on the gravel and then . . .'

Eden released her and ran into the darkened hall and up the stairs towards Gussie's room, her heart pounding, filled with an unspeakable fear.

'Gussie!' She halted in the doorway, panting for breath.

Gussie was sitting at her dressing table, her face a mixture of rage and pain and blinding relief.

'What's happened, Gussie?'

Gussie began to shake. 'He came for me, Eden. He came for me but Allie was here and then you arrived.'

Eden pressed a hand against her palpitating heart. 'Thank God,' she gasped. 'Listen Gussie. Allie has left. I'm staying at St Michel tonight. Tomorrow I'm going for Mae. There won't be another night like this.'

'But there *has* to be, Eden!' Gussie cried fervently. 'He must come for me! I can't stand until I'm old waiting and waiting, not able to love anyone else. A prisoner . . .'

The bottle rattled against the rim of the glass as Eden poured a large brandy.

'If he comes for you, Gussie, you'll die.'

Gussie's tragic eyes met hers. 'I know,' she whispered. 'Oh, Eden! I'm so afraid.'

'So am I,' Eden said truthfully, draining the brandy and pouring another for Gussie.

'Then you believe me? You don't think I'm mad?'

Eden sat unsteadily on the bed, remembering the dark, powerful figure so clearly held in her headlights.

'No,' she said, fighting wave after wave of overwhelming fear. 'I don't think you're mad. I know he's here. I saw him.'

Gussie rushed to the window, opening it wide. 'Beau,' she called vainly. 'Beau! Beau!'

Eden seized her shoulders. 'He mustn't come in, Gussie.'

'But he's in torment. All because of me!'

Their eyes held, wide with terror. Then, like children, they clung together and wept.

CHAPTER SEVEN

They rose before dawn and drank a breakfast of black coffee and Bloody Marys.

'I wish I didn't have to leave you,' Eden said at last, her jacket round her shoulders, car keys in her hand.

'I'll be all right.' There was no conviction in Gussie's voice. It was if she had difficulty concentrating on Eden's presence. Her eyes kept being drawn away from Eden and towards the giant oaks across the dew-wet lawn.

'I'll be back as soon as possible, Gussie.'

'Yes.'

Eden hesitated. It was as if Gussie kept entering another world. Last night, for a brief while, the spell had been broken but now, insidiously, it was back in full force. Cold fingers squeezed Eden's heart. Was it Beau Gussie could see standing beneath the ghostly outline of the oaks? Was he talking to her even now? One thing was certain. If he came for her, Gussie would go as unprotestingly as a bride into the arms of her bridegroom. She would be unable to help herself.

Eden ran to her car. Its tyre marks blazed across several feet of perfectly tended turf. If she needed any evidence of the reality of the events of the previous night, the tyre marks supplied them. She was not highly strung; she was not of a nervous disposition; she was not over-imaginative. What she had seen, she had seen. A tall, lean, powerful figure caught in the headlights of her car as he tried to enter St Michel.

She headed out of New Orleans on the Eastern Express-

153

way. It would be a long haul to Atlanta and she would have to be back by nightfall. She dare not leave Gussie alone in St Michel. She fumbled on the seat beside her for her bag and opened it. Her address book was there, thank God. She could always ring Dr Meredith. At the thought of what exactly she would say to him, she blanched. He wouldn't believe her. She couldn't expect him to. Only Mae would believe her. And Leila Jefferson. Her diary was there as well. She flicked it open and caught her breath. June twenty-second. Nearly a year to the day since they had sat, giggling and light-hearted, in Gussie's bedroom. Was that why Beau was making his presence increasingly felt? Was he waiting for Midsummer's Eve? For the anniversary of his death? She fought down the sobs that rose to her throat. She had to reach Atlanta quickly and she could not do so in a state of near-hysteria. She had to calm down; forget about Beau Clay and concentrate on the road ahead of her.

With relief she left Louisiana and entered Mississippi. It was still early morning and so far she hadn't picked up a ticket for speeding. Not that she gave a damn for tickets. She would probably be festooned with them by the time she reached her destination. All that mattered was that she arrived. Fast. And that Mae return to New Orleans with her.

Gussie, her eyes blank, had watched Eden's car disappear down the drive. Only Eden and Allie had prevented Beau from claiming her. Now Eden was gone and so was Allie. Tonight Beau would triumph. Almost mechanically she walked out into the dawn chill and plucked a rose. No limousine appeared at her side. Had Horatio left St Michel along with Louis and Sabina? Today was important. Today she had to leave her rose at the Clay mausoleum. He would know if she did not do so. He would be angry.

154

Panic seized her. She began to run towards the corner of the white stuccoed mansion, down the side, towards the garage. There was no sign of Horatio. The cars shone sleekly, keys in the ignitions. She opened the door of her Chevrolet. Horatio never left the keys in the car. Doing so was his way of telling her he was leaving. Had left. She reversed into the pale light of dawn. She was sorry Horatio had gone; and Allie. She had liked them. An early-morning paper boy waved blearily to her as she motored towards the city. No one else was about. She was glad. Her dawn visits to the cemetery were private. She wanted no one to see her; no one to intrude. The cemetery was wreathed in a haze that presaged heat. She left the car and walked swiftly towards the ornate magnificence of the Clay tomb.

'*Augusta, Augusta!*' His shadow enveloped her, possessive and demanding.

She stretched her hands out before her but her fingertips met only air.

'Will it be tonight, Beau?' she asked desperately. 'Will you come for me tonight? Will we both be set free?'

'*Augusta* ...' The voice was a faint, vanishing whisper. The shadow was gone.

She began to cry. He gave her so little comfort. She remembered the mocking lines of his mouth, the hint of cruelty. Did he torment her on purpose?

'Oh, Beau,' she wept. 'I'm sorry. I was a child. I didn't realize the enormity of what I was doing.'

The silence taunted her. Dejectedly she left her offering and returned to her car. It was nearly over. Soon he would have his heart's desire. She slid behind the wheel and pushed her hair away from her face. He had been her heart's desire, too. Why, then, did she feel no joy? Why did terror stalk her, rendering her helpless, clouding her mind? Early morning traffic was beginning to pour into the city. She pressed a hand

155

to her throbbing temple and eased her Chevrolet into the empty, northbound lane. It was as if what strength she had possessed had deserted her. She felt weak and tired; too tired to garage the car. She left it, engine still running, door wide open, and made her way to her room and her unmade bed. Allie was beginning to make her absence felt. Uncaringly she drew the crumpled sheets around her shoulders and slept.

The knocking on the door awakened her. She blinked, disorientated. Why didn't someone answer the door? The brass knocker slammed again, the noise reverberating through the empty house. She groaned. Louis had left. Allie had left. There was no one to still the insistent banging but herself.

Reluctantly she hurried bare-footed along the landing, and as the knocking increased in ferocity, ran lightly down the stairs. She would have to give Jim Meredith a key. He still called in each morning. Nothing was achieved by his visits but it kept him happy. Or at least Gussie supposed that it did.

The door was hard to open. She hadn't realized how seldom she opened it for herself. It creaked slightly on its hinges. 'I'm sorry, Jim, I . . .'

Bradley stared down at her.

Her lips parted silently, her eyes widening.

'Going somewhere?' he asked, a distinct edge to his voice as his eyes flicked from her to the Chevrolet.

'Nn . . . no.' She was stammering, blood surging into her cheeks.

His brows rose fractionally.

She had forgotten how tall he was; how broad; how safe he made her feel.

'I've been out. I must have forgotten to turn the engine off.'

'It's still only eight-thirty.' His face was grim. There was no laughter in his eyes, no warmth in his voice.

'Is it? I was up early.'

'You look as if you've just got out of bed,' he said starkly.

Nervously her hand touched her unbrushed hair. For the first time she became aware that she was shoeless.

'I ...' No more words would come.

'Aren't you going to invite me in?'

'I ... No ...' The pain behind her eyes was blinding. 'I must go, Bradley. I'm sorry ...'

She moved to close the door but a strong hand encircled her wrist, holding her fast.

'Has it come to this, Gussie? Slamming the door in my face?'

'No, Bradley. It's just that ... that ...' She floundered helplessly.

'Just what, Gussie? That you don't love me any more? Don't even like me!'

A knife entered her heart and twisted vidently. 'I *do* like you, Bradley. I do ...' She choked, her eyes filling with tears.

'Do what?' he asked savagely. 'Do love me? Say it, Gussie. I want you to say it!'

She felt as if her wrist would break.

'No! I don't love you, Bradley! I don't want to see you! Not ever!'

His brows flew together, his rage murderous. 'I don't believe you, Gussie. What is it with you? Why do you live here all alone? Why are you never seen? Why did Allie run away in the middle of last night?'

She froze, staring up at him like a rabbit at a stoat. 'Allie? How do you know about Allie?'

'Christ!' he said explosively. 'Everyone in the district

157

knows about it by now! She woke the Jefferson household just after midnight. Her mother is cook there. From what Mrs Jefferson says, she was out of her mind with fear. Babbling about black magic, voodoo and spirits from the dead.'

Gussie felt the blood drain from her face. If Jim Meredith heard he would take her away from St Michel by force. Beau would be unable to claim her. She would be locked up in a State institution, tormented by his anguish, by his voice and by his shadow. A fear that was crippling lent her strength.

'She's a fool. You're all fools. Oh God, why won't you leave me alone?'

Her desperation permeated his rage.

'Is it so bad, Gussie?' he asked, his voice suddenly tender.

Her eyes were tortured. 'Please leave me alone,' she whispered. She sagged like a broken doll against the frame of the door, tears coursing down her cheeks.

His voice caught and deepened. 'I can't leave you alone, Gussie. I love you.'

His face was harsh with concern, abrasive in its masculinity.

'I'm going to Houston for two nights. I thought you might like the trip.'

Houston: glass and marble skyscrapers. The Astrodome. Hermann Park. Drinks at Cody's on Montrose.

'No,' she breathed. 'No . . .'

'I'll see you when I get back. I can't take no for an answer, Gussie. I've tried, but I love you too much.'

She stared up at him and froze. When he came back she would no longer be at St Michel. She would be with Beau.

'Yes,' she lied through parched lips. 'I'll see you when you get back. Goodbye, Bradley.'

He stood for several seconds staring at the door as she

closed it behind her. Despite her tears and her insistence that she be left alone, she had agreed to see him again. Reluctantly he turned on his heel and walked across to his Thunderbird, turning off the Chevrolet's engine and closing its door on the way. There was still hope. It would have to suffice for the next forty-eight hours. Heavy-hearted he drove away and headed west.

Eden left Birmingham, Alabama behind her with relief. She was making good time. Another hour and she would be in Georgia. She had purposely not phoned Mae to tell her she was coming. She didn't want to give Mae the opportunity to slip away. She wondered if Gussie was aware of how near Midsummer's Eve was. She hadn't seemed to be. Days, weeks and months seemed to pass by for Gussie in one long, static moment. Eden lit a cigarette and inhaled deeply. Yesterday morning she had wanted Leila Jefferson to convince Gussie that she was letting an obsession ruin her life. Now she wanted Leila for a far more urgent reason: to lay the spirit of Beau Clay to rest. She remembered the tension that had emanated from him in life. His brooding magnetism. He had died because Augusta had summoned him to her side. Gussie's image had been on his brain, her name on his lips as his car had been sucked beneath the surface of the swamp. Dear God. Eden crushed out her cigarette and lit another. What chance did they have of deflecting him from his purpose? It was Gussie herself who had said she wanted Beau to love her forever. Gussie, who, in her foolishness had said that forever was not long enough.

She crossed the State Line into Georgia and looked at her watch. The newly-married Mrs Mae Merriweather had better be home.

'Eden!' Pleasure flooded Mae's plump face,. to be quickly followed by anxiety. 'What is it? Is something the matter? Why didn't you phone?'

'Get your purse,' Eden commanded, whirling round Mae's luxury home, turning off the radio, the coffee percolator, the sprinkler.

'But why? Have you gone mad? You must be dying for a drink after that long drive. I have some Chablis . . .'

'There's no time for Chablis,' Eden said grimly.

Mae stared at her, stunned. Coming from Eden such a statement was blasphemous.

'None of your damned family are remotely co-operative. I wanted to get hold of your grandmother and they won't even tell me where the Jefferson house is. I spent all yesterday lost in swamps and marshland.'

Mae stumbled and sat down heavily, her rosy cheeks ashen. 'It's Gussie, isn't it?'

'Too damned right, it's Gussie,' Eden said, closing doors and windows. 'You'd better phone Austin and tell him you'll be away for a couple of nights.'

'But I can't do that,' Mae began.

Eden whipped round on her, her eyes flaming. 'You'd better do, Mae Merriweather. Your silly ritual has already taken one life. I'm not going to let it take Gussie's!'

'I don't know what you mean,' Mae whispered, taking the telephone as Eden thrust it into her hand.

'It's killed Beau Clay and it's killing Gussie, daily – by inches.'

Mae gasped for breath. 'Beau's death was an accident.'

Eden stood over her, frightening in her intensity. 'An accident caused because he was racing to Gussie's side. He died only seconds after we left St Michel. You know that, Mae. You've known it all along. You knew he was driving towards New Orleans at such a suicidal speed because Gussie

160

had summoned him. How, only God and your grandmother know, and perhaps even God has been left in the dark.'

Mae shrunk back against the cushions on the sofa. 'Don't say such things, Eden. Don't! Don't!'

'Phone Austin,' Eden ordered.

Reluctantly Mae did as she was bid. '. . . dreadfully sorry, darling. My grandmother's ill. I'll be back in a couple of days. . . . I love you too . . .'

Mae's voice was tear-filled enough to convince Austin that her grandmother was on the point of death. As she made her stumbling excuses Eden grabbed rolls and biscuits. There would be no time to stop on the return trip and she couldn't remember when she had last eaten.

'I'm not an hysteric. If I say I saw him, I saw him,' Eden said as they headed south.

Mae moaned and hugged her arms. 'Why did we ever do it, Eden? I knew something awful would happen.'

'No, you didn't. You were going to do it yourself. You were going to bind Bradley Hampton to you forever.'

'Oh God,' Mae's teeth chattered uncontrolably. 'It was only a joke . . .'

'It isn't a joke now.'

'No.' .

They lapsed into silence, hardly speaking until Birmingham was in sight. Eden left the highway for a service station and filled the tank.

'I'm going to make a couple of phone calls.'

'Who to?'

'Bradley Hampton and Dr Meredith.'

Five minutes later she was back in the Cadillac, her face grim.

'We're on our own, Mae Merriweather, whether we like it or not. Bradley is in Houston and Jim Meredith has taken his wife to Fort Lauderdale.'

'There won't be time,' Mae said unhappily as the signposts for Meridian, Mississippi flashed by them. 'It's near dark now and the plantation is impossible to find at night. It's surrounded by swamps and forests.'

Eden didn't argue with her. She knew very well the kind of country that surrounded the Jefferson plantation.

'As long as we're both with her, it won't matter,' she said, wishing she could sound more confident. 'Besides, I don't think anything will happen tonight.'

'Why not?'

'Because tonight isn't Midsummer's Eve. Tomorrow night is.'

'*Oh God!*' May gasped again and began to cry.

'Bradley came this morning,' Gussie said with unnerving calm as Eden and Mae sprawled exhaustedly on the sofas. She paused as she poured a drink. 'I could have been happy married to Bradley.'

Eden demolished a tuna sandwich and drained a glass of ice-cold Chablis. 'Sleeping pills,' she said, handing Gussie a couple. 'Mae and I don't need them. Not after the day we've had. But you do. We'll see Mae's grandmother tomorrow. All three of us will go together.'

She expected a protest from Gussie and was surprised when none came. Gussie swallowed them calmly, her composure disconcerting.

'I never realized before how *big* this house is,' Mae said as a moth fluttered against the window pane of the twenty-roomed colonial mansion.

'Don't you get awful lonely, Gussie?'

'No,' Gussie said, her hair gleaming pale-gold in the lamplight. 'I'm never alone, Mae. Beau is with me. Always.'

'Stop talking like that!' Eden said sharply.

Gussie's eyes were bleak. 'Why? It's the truth, Eden. You know. You've seen him.'

'We need to get to bed and to sleep,' Eden said tersely, regarding sleep as a short cut to morning. 'I'll sleep on the sofa in your room, Gussie. Mae can sleep . . .'

'I'm not sleeping on my own! I'll sleep on the floor with you two, but I'm not sleeping on my own!'

Pillows and duvets from other rooms were gathered together and laid on the floor and sofa in Gussie's bedroom. Mae was talking about Austin, calming down after her near-hysteria. Eden watched them, a frown creasing her forehead. Gussie was unnaturally quiet; resigned almost. The only time her eyes had not been expressionless had been when she'd mentioned Bradley's name. Remembering the lamp that had burned in the window for Beau the previous evening, Eden insisted that they slept in darkness. Mae was reluctant and kept fear at bay by chattering about Austin; about the new house; about how they wanted a baby straight away; about how happy she was. Hearing Gussie's polite responses, Eden felt a measure of relief. She had been right to bring Mae back with her. Right to insist they all spent the night at St Michel. Against her will, her lids closed and she drifted off to sleep.

'So Austin said . . .' Mae continued drowsily. '. . . Austin thought . . .'

In the darkness Gussie waited. It was sweet of Eden to go to such lengths to save her from her own fate. She had not even minded when Eden had returned from Atlanta with Mae. She had known that their presence would make little difference.

'*Augusta*.' Her name floated gently over the sleeping bodies of her friends.

'*Augusta*.'

Slowly she slipped out of the bed and stepped over Mae.

With sure fingers she lit the oil lamp that was a Lafayette legacy and placed it on the table near the window. In the flickering light the eyes of her dolls gleamed. She touched them fondly, rearranging a skirt here, an arm there. Then she crossed to the dressing table and began to brush her hair in long, rhythmic strokes.

Attracted by the light, moths beat frantically on the window pane. Eden turned in her sleep and sighed. Gussie lay down her silver-backed hairbrush and walked softly to the door, opening it and letting the lamplight illuminate the darkness beyond.

'Soon,' she whispered, her heart beating so fast she could hardly breathe. 'Soon, dear love.'

She crossed to the wardrobe, searching through the dresses with trembling hands. Her fingers touched lace and she drew in a deep, shuddering breath. Her wedding dress. That was what Beau had been waiting for. He had been wanting her to meet him as a bride. *His* bride, not Bradley Hampton's. She paused, light-headed, unable to think clearly.

Bradley? Did she love Bradley too? She tried to conjure up his face but at the effort the blood pounded in her ears. Beau's image swam before her, an amber flame burning deep in his eyes. The lines of his mouth were hard and savage and jealous.

'Beau!' she called out helplessly. 'Oh Beau! Beau!'

It was like being poised on the edge of eternity. She felt dizzy, sick with fear and longing. Beads of perspiration broke out on her forehead as she slipped the lace over her head and shoulders, smoothing down the bodice, the underskirts rustling as the lace settled over them.

'*I'm ready, Beau!*' Her heart began to slam in heavy, thick strokes. The blood coursed through her veins so hotly that she felt she was on fire.

'*Beau*! . . .'

There came, unmistakeable, the sound of footsteps on gravel.

'What the . . .' Eden said, her eyes flickering open, widening instantaneously. '*No, Gussie!*' she yelled, leaping to her feet. '*No! No!*'

Gussie smiled at her, raising a finger to her lips to silence her.

'Goodbye, Eden.'

'*No!*' Eden threw herself forward but Gussie was beyond her grasp, moving out onto the landing as the heavy knocker slammed at the door.

'Oh God!' Mae screamed, sitting up wild-eyed. 'What is it? *Oh Gussie!* GUSSIE!'

The knocker fell again.

'*I'm coming, Beau!*' Gussie called, her skirts in her hands as she ran down the broad curving sweep of the staircase. '*I'm coming, sweet love!*'

Eden leaned on the banisters, panting. Gussie was nearly at the foot of the stairs. Through the glass panels of the door a dark silhouetted figure stood, waiting for admittance. The knocker fell again, impatient; insistent.

'I'm coming . . .'

With superhuman strength Eden wrenched the enormous, gilt-framed mirror from the wall behind her and flung it with all her might over the banisters, sending it crashing between Gussie's running figure and the terrifying silhouette of Beau Clay.

Gussie's shriek was ear-piercing. Glass and wood splintered and flew. For a mind-searing second Eden thought she had killed her. Mae screamed and continued to scream as Eden stumbled and fell down the crimson-carpeted stairs to where Gussie lay senseless on the marble floor.

'Gussie!' she cried urgently, feeling her pulse, sobbing

with relief at the light, rapid beat beneath her fingertips. *'Gussie!'*

Gussie's lids moved fractionally. Eden swung her head towards the door, drenched in the cold perspiration of fear.

Through the glass panels the moon shone clearly: not even a shadow darkening its path.

'He's gone, Mae,' she said shakily. 'Come down and help me with Gussie.'

Emerging from the door of the bedroom and walking down the dark staircase was the bravest thing Mae had ever done. 'What are we going to do?' she whispered shakily as Eden slapped Gussie's cheeks. 'Dear God, Eden. What are we going to *do*?'

Gussie's eyes flickered open.

'He's gone,' Eden said, her voice breaking.

'I know.' She looked up at them dazedly. 'He's gone to Houston for two days. He wanted me to go with him, but I couldn't. Why are you looking at me so strangely, Eden?'

'Let's get her to bed,' Eden said, sliding her arm round Gussie's waist.

'Why couldn't I go with him? I can't remember.'

'One step at a time,' Eden said as they began to mount the stairs.

'My head feels so strange, Eden. As if I'd been flying.'

'We're nearly there.'

Gussie halted, staring down at her wedding gown, realization dawning, horror engulfing her. 'Oh, no! Oh dear God! No! *No!*'

Eden fumbled for the light switch in Gussie's bedroom, plunging them into brilliance. Gussie's eyes were dilated, her face contorted with fear, her breath coming in harsh gasps. 'He's coming for me! He'll find me wherever I am!'

Eden grasped her arms, shaking her viciously. 'It's *over*, Gussie. For tonight it's over.'

Gussie sank on to the bed, hugging her arms, rocking backwards and forwards. 'He wants me, Eden. He wants me forever!'

With a trembling hand Eden pushed the hair away from her face and sat on the dressing-table stool. Mae sat on the floor, her knees pulled up to her chin, crying quietly.

'Why do you go to him?' Eden asked unsteadily, wishing she had the strength to pour a drink; light a cigarette; anything.

'He calls me.' The rocking ceased. She sat very still. 'He calls me and I feel as if I'm drowning in his voice. I can see only him. Only Beau. Other people cease to matter. Even Bradley . . .'

'Stop it, Gussie!' Eden leapt to her feet and slapped Gussie's face hard.

Gussie stared up at her in shocked amazement.

'You're letting him hypnotize you!'

'He wants me,' Gussie said simply. 'He won't rest until we're together.'

Eden's eyes sparked flames. 'He's not going to have you, Gussie! To go to him means going to your death!'

Gussie moaned, rubbing her goose-fleshed arms. 'What am I to do, Eden? He's waiting for me. Every night he comes to St Michel, waiting to be let in.' Her voice rose dazedly. 'Waiting to take me . . .'

'Let's get you out of that dress,' Eden said authoritatively, stemming the tide of hysteria. 'Mae, stop crying and help me.'

Unresisting, Gussie allowed them to remove the wedding dress and slip a negligé over her head and shoulders.

'We need coffee,' Eden said, 'strong and black.'

They looked at each other, aware that no one was on call:

167

that the house was bereft of staff. Eden's eyes rested on Mae.

Mae shook her head vigorously. 'I'm not going down to make coffee. I'd rather die first.'

Eden sighed. 'Will you be all right, Gussie, if I leave you with Mae?'

Gussie nodded.

Eden took a deep breath and then, singing 'Onward Christian Soldiers' gustily at the top of her voice, made her way down the stairs and through the house to the kitchen, switching on every light she passed.

'I never want to spend another night like that as long as I live,' Mae said next morning as they huddled over Bloody Marys in the sun-filled kitchen.

Eden drained her glass. 'This is a habit I'll have to break. Vodka and tomato juice at seven in the morning is too much for even me.'

Gussie said only, 'I'm scared. Oh God, how I'm scared.'

'You and me, too,' Eden said, rising to her feet. 'Come on. Let's go.'

They drove out of the city on Highway 10, Eden at the wheel, heading south towards the Cajun country where long ago Mae's ancestors had settled.

'I hate it,' Mae said. 'It's all alligators, swamps and marshes. My mother always said my great-grandfather must have had a dreadful secret to hide, living so far away from civilization.'

'Your grandmother can't hate it,' Eden said, glancing uneasily at Gussie who had once more lapsed into silence. 'What do you think, Gussie?'

'About what?' Gussie's eyes held the bleak expression that Eden had learned to be wary of.

'Mae's grandmother. She can't hate living where she does or she wouldn't live there, would she?'

'No.' Gussie's hands twisted in her lap. Leila Jefferson. Would she be able to free her from Beau? She shivered. If Leila Jefferson could not help her, no one could.

She blinked back the tears that filled her eyes. Why had she done it? Why had she been so foolish and naïve? Beau Clay had never been destined for her. He had been destined for someone as reckless, as heedless as himself. She didn't want an exciting, fast-living lover who didn't give a flying damn about anyone or anything. She wanted tenderness: strength; stability. A home of her own, and babies. She clenched her hands tightly together. She wanted things Beau Clay could never have given her. She wanted Bradley.

'Are you O.K., Gussie?' Mae asked nervously.

'Yes. Fine,' Gussie lied.

If only she hadn't been so headstrong; so impatient for love. If only she had waited a little longer . . . With anguished eyes she stared unseeingly at the signpost for Crowley. Beau would eventually have been forgotten. Bradley would have succeeded him in her thoughts and her dreams. Bradley, who loved her of his own volition. Who needed no Midsummer's Eve ceremony to be awakened to her existence. Dear God. Panic welled up in her. Instead of waiting for love to find her, she had demanded it and now it was destroying her. Beau Clay had never been refused anything in life, and he was not going to be refused anything in death. She was his. Just as she had wanted to be. His, forever and forever and forever.

She began to cry softly and Mae leaned forward from the back seat and laid a hand compassionately on her shoulder.

'Don't cry, Gussie. It'll be all right. Just see if it won't.'

'Is that the turn-off for Jennings?' Eden asked, blinking against the sun.

'Yes,' Mae replied unhappily. 'We need to take Exit 27. It'll be coming up in another few minutes.'

'I'm not surprised your mother hardly visits,' Eden said as she turned off the highway and headed south towards the Gulf. 'It isn't exactly the bright lights, is it?'

'It gets worse,' Mae said, leaning forward. 'We branch off here.'

'That's barely a road.'

'It's the one we take.'

Raucous birds flew out of the undergrowth, screeching at their intrusion. Trees hemmed them in, draped in trailing fronds of Spanish moss, the ground gleaming slickly at their roots.

'Swamp,' Mae said unnecessarily. 'Left again.'

'For goodness' sake, Mae. No wonder I couldn't find your damned plantation on my own. Doesn't anyone believe in road signs around here?'

'Left again,' Mae said mercilessly. 'We're nearly there.'

The house had been glorious once, surrounded on all sides by gleaming white columns and balconies. Now the paint was peeling and flaked and tropical vegetation had surged over what had once been lawns. Wild roses, lilies, lavender and wild jasmine invaded the open windows of the lower rooms, their perfume lingering in the hot, airless, heat.

'No one *makes* her live here,' Mae said helplessly, as they climbed out of the Cadillac. 'You can see why my mother doesn't encourage visitors.'

There was a sudden start, quickly suppressed, in the eyes of the elderly maid who opened the door to them.

'Is Grandma home, Louella?'

Dark, unfathomable eyes flicked from Mae's tear-stained face, over Eden; and rested on Gussie.

'She's out on the back gallery.'

The spicy aroma of chicken simmering with garlic and herbs and red peppers filled the air. Cicadas sang in the dense surrounding foliage as old eyes met young. The shadows beneath Gussie's eyes were dark, like bruises, the expression tormented. The old Black woman nodded her head imperceptibly. To Eden it seemed as if they had been expected. As if the stooped, wrinkled figure before them knew Augusta's identity without being told. A tremor ran down her spine. Was the woman before them a *voodooienne*? If so, surely that was why they had come? She licked her lips and tried to control her fear.

'It's hot,' Louella said. 'You'll be needing drinks. I'll bring them out to you.' The voice was flat. Expressionless. Uncomfortably they moved past her and into shadow inside.

The house possessed a genteel air of decay. The polished floors gleamed dully through a fine layer of dust, the scatter rugs on their surface faded and worn. There was no modern air-conditioning. Old-fashioned fans creaked and whirred, merging with the never-ending sounds from the encroaching forest and swamps. Insects buzzed incessantly. A small lizard ran across the floor and disappeared down a crack in the boards.

The furniture was sturdy: mahogany and oak; furniture that had survived from colonial days. The damask and velvet upholstery, once so rich and glowing, now barely showed any colour but sun-faded beige. There were books on the wall shelves, flowers on the tables. The waxy white of magnolias, the scarlet of bougainvillea, the flowering pink tentacles of Queen's Wreath. All the flowers of the encroaching wilderness had been brought inside so that the rooms seemed bottled in green-tinted light. Round an open window mosquito nets hung limply and a luxuriant creeper penetrated beneath the netting and into the room, trailing over the back of a chair so that at first glance it was impossible to see where the room ended and the undergrowth began.

There was an air of shabby comfort that Gussie had not expected. Perhaps Leila Jefferson was not as unreasonable as she seemed in not living dutifully with her son and daughter-in-law.

The heat rose in waves. Gussie could feel her blouse sticking to her skin, damp with perspiration. A dog began to bark frenziedly at their approach, and Eden flinched. As they neared the door leading on to the vast gallery the dog ran towards them, glassy-eyed and angry.

'It's me, Houla,' Mae said reassuringly. 'Here boy, friend.'

The Catahoula Leopard dog growled warningly as Mae stretched out her hand and allowed it to sniff.

'Good boy. Good dog.' Mae's hand moved tentatively to the top of its spotted head. The growling stopped and its tail began to move suspiciously.

'He's all right,' said Mae to a nervous Eden and Gussie. 'Just making sure of us, that's all. He's the best hunting dog there is.'

Gussie gave him a wide berth and they stepped out on to the back gallery.

'Heaven help us, what a surprise!' the old lady in the rocking chair exclaimed, rising to her feet, her eyes bright, a delighted smile on her face as she held her arms out to her granddaughter.

'Hi, Gran.' Mae ran towards her, hugged her, and at the bodily contact her hysteria could be controlled no longer. Her voice broke and she began to cry.

Leila Jefferson regarded her in total astonishment. 'Mae. What is it? Is there trouble at home? Is anyone ill . . . ?'

'No, Gran. No. Everyone's just fine in town,' Mae said, struggling to control her breathing, to speak rationally.

'But there is trouble. The most awful, unimaginable trouble ...'

Unsteadily Leila Jefferson sank back down into her rocking chair, her hands still grasping Mae's.

'Is it that husband of yours, child? He seemed like a real fine boy.'

Mae shook her head. 'No, Gran. It's not Austin. It's ... It's Gussie.'

Eden and Gussie had halted at the glass-panelled doorway as Mae had greeted her grandmother. Eden was surprised at how sane and normal the figure of New Orleans' voodoo gossip looked in the flesh. Her hair was still dark; still thick. She wore it as she had done as a girl, piled high on her head, long jet earrings hanging against a jawline that was no longer firm but still held traces of beauty. Leila Jefferson, Eden thought, must have been a stunner in her youth. No wonder she was still remembered and talked about.

Gussie had been too tense with anticipation to notice anything at all about the petite, almost dainty figure in the rocking chair. And then Mae spoke her name and Leila Jefferson froze, ageing before them, her gaiety fleeing, her delight at Mae's visit a a thing of the past.

'Gussie?' she asked, and her voice was little more than a whisper. 'Gussie Lafayette?'

'Yes, Gran. She's ...'

Leila Jefferson's hands released Mae's. Her eyes moved beyond her granddaughter to where Gussie stood with Eden. Not for one second did her eyes rest on Eden.

'So it happened,' she said, and Eden felt fear surge up and swamp her. 'It happened as I knew it would.'

'Gran ...'

Slowly Leila Jefferson rose to her feet and faced Gussie.

'The same hair, the same eyes, the same face ...' Her

words trailed away. She remained standing, one arm on the rocking chair for support, staring at Gussie.

Eden fought to control her fear. Perhaps Leila Jefferson *was* crazy. Too crazy to help them. Perhaps no one *could* help them.

'Poor Chantel, thinking she could escape so easily.' The old lady's hand reached out and took Gussie's and Gussie began to cry. Leila Jefferson wrapped her arms around her, hushing her as if she were a child.

'What vengeance is Loa exacting, child?'

Mae was confused. 'I don't know what you mean, Gran. It's not a god. It's not even voodoo. Not really. At least ...' she faltered. '... it didn't seem like voodoo at the time. It was a joke: a silly, stupid joke.'

Leila Jefferson had returned to her chair, and Gussie knelt at her side, their hands still clasped.

'Nothing to do with Loa can be taken lightly. It may have seemed like a joke, Mae, but Loa has waited a long time for revenge.'

Mae shook her head desperately. Was her Gran going to fail them after all? Rambling on about her voodoo god without even listening to the story of Midsummer's Eve and without even knowing about Beau Clay?

'I don't know what you're talking about, Gran. We don't know anyone called Loa. It's Gussie who is in trouble. Gussie who needs help.'

Leila Jefferson sighed and it was the deep, tearing sigh of old age and final capitulation.

'Whatever trouble Gussie Lafayette is in, is because of Loa. He's waited half a century for revenge and I've lived half a century in fear of it.' She looked down at Gussie. 'Tell me, child. What did you do to open the doors to the spirits?'

Eden stood so still she could hear her own heartbeat above the sound of the encircling insects. Mae sat silently, wiping the tears from her cheeks. Louella came to the door with a tray of iced drinks and halted, listening, her eyes full of pain.

'It was Midsummer's Eve a year ago,' Gussie said with strange calm as she felt the strength of Leila Jefferson's handhold. 'Mae said she'd heard you speak of a Midsummer's Eve ceremony where you could make the boy you loved, love you.'

Imperceptibly Leila Jefferson's dark head nodded.

'I ... wanted someone very badly. More than anything.' She paused. Where was he now? Surely he knew what she was doing? That she was betraying him? Her throat was dry. The words came with difficulty.

'I wrote his name backwards on paper and at midnight, looking into the mirror, I ate it and I wished and wished with all my might, mind and strength that I might have him. That he would love me as I loved him.' The last word was barely audible. 'Forever.'

Leila's eyes held hers. It was as if Mae and Eden were not present. 'Who's name did you write, child?'

The answer came in a long, drawn-out breath from the centre of her being. 'Beauregard Clay.'

No one moved or spoke. Trailing greenery around them seemed to draw nearer, suffocating them in its fronds and tendrils.

At last, after a long time, Mae said quietly, 'He died, Gran. Minutes after midnight on Midsummer's Eve, he died driving his car at breakneck speed to Gussie's home.'

'And his body and spirit no longer inhabit his tomb.' It was Leila Jefferson's voice, and it was not a question. Just a statement of fact.

'He's coming for me,' Gussie said simply. 'He wants me to join him: to honour the vow I made. To be his forever and forever ... Beyond the grave.'

175

In the silence that followed a brown pelican flapped its wings and emerged from beneath the surrounding density of oaks and water, a struggling fish trapped in its beak. Something unseen scurried across the floor behind them and disappeared. A spider skimmed down a length of thread and hung, blue-black, in the air above them.

It was as if Leila Jefferson already knew. None of the arguments Eden had mentally prepared had to be put forward.

'I stayed at St Michel with Gussie,' Eden said, speaking for the first time. 'We'd had a tiring day and fell asleep quickly. When we woke . . .' She hesitated and looked across at Gussie's marble-white face. 'When we woke Gussie was wearing her wedding gown and was standing in the middle of the room. There was a lamp lit at the window and the door was open.' She licked dry lips. 'There were footsteps on the gravel outside. Both Mae and I heard them. Gussie was radiant. She really did look like a bride. It was as if she were lit by an inner flame. The knocker fell and we could see him clearly, silhouetted in a glass panel. Gussie began to run down the stairs and Mae began to scream and the knocker slammed again and again . . .' Eden broke off, trembling convulsively.

'What did you do?' Leila Jefferson asked steadily.

Eden clenched her hands together to still them. 'I wrenched a mirror off the wall and threw it down between Gussie and the door.'

'And then?'

Eden shook her head purposefully. 'I don't know. I didn't see him go. I thought I'd killed Gussie. There was glass and wood everywhere and Gussie was unconscious. When she came round she didn't know what had happened. Not at first. When she remembered she was terrified. She said that

176

Beau would not rest until she joined him. That there was no way she could escape him.'

There was infinite sadness in Leila Jefferson's voice. 'A harmless prank. And because of Chantel . . . this. Because of me.'

The three girls stared at her, not understanding.

For a few seconds she was lost in a reverie they could not enter. And then she visibly shook herself and turned to the still figure in the doorway.

'I think we'll be having those drinks now, Louella, if you please.'

Only when the drinks had revived them and Louella had replenished their glasses did anyone speak, Gussie the first, venturing to ask what she had wanted to know all her life.

'My grandmother, Chantel, what was she like? Why should any of this be her fault. Or yours?'

Leila's eyes were suspiciously bright as she looked down at the living likeness kneeling beside her chair.

'Chantel Gallière was the prettiest, kindest and liveliest girl in New Orleans. We were friends from our cradles. We played together; laughed together; dreamed dreams together.'

Tears sparkled on her lashes.

'And then one night I led her to her death.' She no longer saw the three girls before her. She was back again in the hot, sultry night of her youth. Hearing Chantel plead to turn back; to go home. Once again deep in the darkened forest, water gleaming malevolently between the cypress-shrouded trees, their way made barely passable by the sluggishly flowing bayous.

'Then it was an accident? She didn't drown herself?' Gussie asked feveredly.

For a second she wondered if Leila Jefferson had heard her, and then Leila said, with a strange catch to her voice,

177

'No, child. It was no accident. She walked out of her home and into the forest. And when she found water deep enough she walked out into it and spread herself face down upon it and died.'

'But why?' Gussie's eyes were huge, anguished.

'Because she had taken part in a voodoo ritual. She was a bride of the god Loa. As I was. And she couldn't live with that burden. She thought it a burden that could be laid down but I knew differently. To lay it down is to invite revenge. Loa could not strike through her child, a son. He has had to wait as long as I have had to wait. He has had to wait for you. A daughter of Chantel's blood.'

Gussie stared at her, round-eyed. 'But my grandmother wouldn't ... Not voodoo ...'

Leila's eyes held pain so deep that Eden felt her spine tingle. 'When I was a girl, Louella was my maid. A *voodienne*. One night we followed her when she left my father's house. Chantel was frightened of the dark and asked me to go back ... To return home. But I said "no". If we turned back we would get lost in the swamp. That we had to go on.' Her body sank against the cushions of her chair, frail and defeated. 'Louella was going to a ceremony. A ceremony to give power over a dead spirit. And we were found. I thought that we were going to be killed. Then Louella intervened and pleaded that we be made brides of Loa, a voodoo god. As such we would never be able to tell what we had seen or participated in, for to do so would be to call down Loa's wrath. I didn't believe in voodoo then. I thought it a childish, ridiculous ceremony. I was to learn later of my ignorance and stupidity. Chantel was never so foolish. She realized the horror she had committed herself to. And she escaped by death.'

'Leaving me to face Loa's revenge?' The breath in Gussie's chest was so tight she could scarcely utter the words.

'I'm afraid so, child. Sooner or later Loa would have destroyed your life in revenge for the bride who broke her vow. Your silly, harmless little Midsummer's Eve ceremony was ideally suited for the purpose. Your death for Chantel's.'

Gussie's voice was taut with pain. 'And Beau? Is he bound to Loa too?'

Leila Jefferson shook her head. 'No, child. Beauregard Clay is a spirit in torment. Bound not to Loa but to you through the ceremony you enacted. The ceremony that Loa lent power to for his own ends. The ceremony that your own, obsessive love made possible.'

'How do we free them?' It was Eden's voice, seeming to Gussie to come from light years away. 'How do we free Gussie from Loa's power? How do we free Beau so that he may sleep in peace?'

Leila Jefferson looked down at Gussie's upturned face. 'Do you believe with all your soul that you *can* free yourself from the powers of darkness?'

'Yes.' The answer came unhesitatingly, strong and firm.

'Do you believe that a reversal of the ceremony you enacted will free Beau from you?'

'Yes.' ·

Gussie's eyes held Leila's unflinchingly.

A tremor ran through Leila's body and was stilled.

'Good.'

'But what of Loa?' Eden said hesitantly. 'How will he be appeased?'

'He will be appeased, child. There is not one Loa, but numberless Loas. So I have learned in the years since Chantel's death. And I have learned how such supernatural forces can be placated. It needs voodoo to combat voodoo.'

When she had told them what they must do, she smiled suddenly at them: a devastatingly pretty smile for such an aged face. 'This is why I have lived as I have. Waiting for the day when my knowledge can atone for Chantel's death and free her descendants from the curse my foolishness brought upon them.'

'But Gran. . . .' Mae began to protest.

'No more questions, Mae. What I do, I do alone. What you do, you must do together.'

A flush of rose tinged the sky. Eden held out her hand and grasped Leila's. 'We must be going. There isn't much time. We'll come back afterwards to thank you properly.'

The smile on Leila's face held a touch of sadness. She would not be there when they returned. Her life, lived solely for the day that was now coming to a close, was nearly over. She would not live to see another sunrise. Not after the ceremony she would enact that night.

'Goodbye, Mrs Jefferson,' Gussie said, her confidence returned. 'Thank you for telling me all about my grandmother and of how pretty and kind she was. Thank you for telling me what to do. Thank you for doing whatever it is you have to do.' She bent forward to kiss Leila on the cheek. 'I shall never forget. Never.'

Mae hugged her grandmother goodbye and then they were gone, running through the jungle of tropical vegetation to the rutted track and their car.

The gold hoops in Louella's ears glinted in the late afternoon sun.

'I reckon our waiting time is over, Miss Leila,' she said as the car bucketed into the thick forest of oak and cypress.

'Yes,' Leila said, feeling the silence and dusk settle around her. 'The waiting is finally over.'

CHAPTER EIGHT

'Will it work?' Mae asked tentatively as the wilderness of knotted figs and knife-blade banana and wild roses was left behind and they headed towards New Orleans.

'For Christ's sake!' Eden said, bucking down the seldom-used track to the highway. 'It *has* to work.'

She flicked an anxious look across at Gussie. The last thing she wanted was for doubt to enter Gussie's mind. If it did, the ceremony that was to be enacted would be worthless. Only overwhelming belief would lend it power.

'It will work,' Gussie said tersely, her face harrowed at the thought of the ordeal ahead. 'Quickly, Eden. It's getting dark. I don't want to be away from St Michel in the dark.'

Mae's bottom lip trembled. She could not endure another night like the previous one. 'Can I go home now? I can stay with my mother this evening and . . .'

'*No!*' Eden's voice was explosive. 'You were in this affair at the beginning, Mae. You're going to see it through.'

Mae choked back a sudden onrush of tears and leaned back in her seat, oblivious as they made the highway and Eden increased speed.

Gussie sank into silence as the late afternoon sun reddened with the first tints of dusk. Beau knew her mind; her very thoughts. He would do everything in his power to prevent her from severing the bond that held her to him. Always before, whenever she had thought of Bradley, or had contemplated leaving her self-imposed incarceration at St Michel, he had come to her in full force. Possessive and jealous; determined that she should belong to no one but him. What would he do now when he knew she was preparing to free herself forever? She felt sick with fear and apprehension. She must not think of him. She must not allow his voice to enter her mind. She must fight his presence with all her strength.

For the moment there was no need. He was strangely silent. Where was he, her demon lover? Was he laughing at her pathetic attempt at freedom? His lips curved in the sardonic smile she had come to know so well? His black eyes glittering mockingly? She shivered. He would not let her go easily. It would be a battle of wills, hers against his. If she won she would be able to pick up the pieces of her life – marry Bradley and be happy as Mae was happy: live uneventfully and joyfully with children and grandchildren. If she lost . . .

If she lost she would bound throughout eternity to the menacing, overpowering figure that haunted her. There would be no warmth; no children. Only the obsessive uniting of two people who, in life, had never exchanged a kiss in love. There would be only death.

'We'll stay with you every minute,' Eden was saying. 'There's nothing to be frightened of, Gussie.'

Mae summed up a shred of bravery. 'We're lucky really,' she said unconvincingly. 'If it wasn't Midsummer's Eve we wouldn't be able to do anything.'

Her words did not comfort her listeners. They knew that it was not coincidence that Beau Clay had materialized with such ferocity the previous evening. It had been a preparation for the anniversary of his death; for the night when he intended seizing Gussie's heart and soul and dragging her beyond the grave to his own tortured world.

The blue haze of twilight was clouding the trees of St Michel as they speeded up the drive. Mae fought the impulse to plead for release and scurry to her parents. She had a responsibility towards Gussie; the whole nightmare had been of her doing. Faint-heartedly she stumbled from the car in Eden's wake.

Gussie glanced over her shoulder and across the darkening lawn to the giant oaks.

'No!' Eden's shout scared Mae nearly out of her wits. 'Don't look over there, Gussie! Don't give him a chance to enter your mind!'

She seized hold of Gussie and ran with her up the shallow steps between the graceful pillars, fumbling with key and lock. The heavy door slammed shut behind them. The house, previously so warm and friendly, was permeated with silence and sadness.

'Music,' Eden said briskly. 'Put on tapes, records, radios, TVs – the lot.'

Mae hurried to do her bidding, glad to be able to blank out the stillness that held the house in thrall.

'What do we need?' Eden asked.

'Alcohol,' Mae said as George Benson and Stevie Wonder fought for supremacy against the background commentary of a baseball match.

'That's one thing we're not going to indulge in,' Eden said grimly. 'We're going to need our wits about us. Alcohol can wait.'

'Needles,' Gussie said nervously. 'Needles and paper.'

'That's simple enough. It could have been eye of newt and toe of frog.'

'Stop it, Eden,' Mae said, biting her nails. 'How can you joke about it?'

'I'm not joking,' Eden said, leading them into the kitchen and plugging in the percolator. 'We're going to sit in here and talk about anything and everything. But *not* Beau Clay. And not what has to be done later this evening. I don't want to give him the merest chance of making his presence felt. If he does, Gussie will weaken and the battle will be lost before it's begun.' She delved in the fridge for cream. 'You can start the ball rolling by telling us about your honeymoon, Mae. Does Austin wear his glasses to make love? I've always wondered.'

"This is the Seven o'Clock Show. Our guests tonight are ..." In a distant room the television could be heard at full volume.

'*Augusta.*' It was so faint as to be almost indiscernible.

"Our first guest this evening is ..."

'*Augusta.*'

Gussie spilt coffee in a long steaming stream across the table.

'*Augusta. Let me in. I'm waiting for you. Augusta ...*'

'*No!*' Violently she pushed her chair away from the table, covering her ears with her hands, her eyes wild. 'No! Go away! I won't listen! I won't!'

Eden leapt to her feet, dragging Mae with her.

'Link hands and sing "The Star-Spangled Banner", *loud*.'

Through the empty rooms of St Michel their voices rang incongruously. Eden's stridently loud; Mae's terrified but with increasing vigour; Gussie's desperate.

'Oh! Say, does that star-spangled banner yet wave
O'er the land of the free, and the home of the brave ...'

They paused for breath and Gussie launched frantically into the remaining verses, to be joined rapidly by the others.

'... and the star-spangled banner in triumph shall wave
O'er the land of the free and the home of the brave ...'

As the last notes died away, Mae and Eden stared tensely

184

at Gussie. She sank back onto her chair with relief. 'It's all right. He's gone.'

'Did I ever tell you about the time I went to Florida with Jason Shreve's father?' Eden asked, setting a silver biscuit barrel in the centre of the table.

'Eden Alexander! You didn't!' Mae exclaimed, shocked.

Eden grinned. 'I did, and very enjoyable it was. There's a lot to be said in favour of older men.'

On the stereo Stevie Wonder gave way to David Bowie and then Elton John. 'It's nearly nine o'clock,' Mae said, as Eden made fresh coffee.

'We're not going upstairs until the last minute,' Eden said decisively. 'That bedroom is filled with Beau's presence. It would be like walking into the lion's den. Is it true your aunt Tina has her maid iron her stockings? She must burn a dozen pairs a week.'

The hands on the large kitchen clock crept round from nine to nine-thirty and from nine-thirty to ten.

'. . . so Dean will be in Los Angeles until the fall and then we'll get married . . .'

'*Augusta*' There was urgent demand in the whisper. '*Augusta! Listen to me . . .*'

'Oh God, no! Please leave me!'

She was stumbling to her feet. Eden and Mae grabbed her arms.

'"Rock of Ages",' Eden panted, marching Gussie up and down the chrome-and-glass fitted kitchen, singing as fervently as any Salvationist.

At last they stood silent and Gussie began to cry. 'He's gone, but he'll come back, Eden. He won't be beaten so easily.'

Eden fought the desire for a large brandy. 'If he can be kept at bay until you sit at the dressing table, then he can be beaten. I never thought I'd sing that wretched thing again.

It was my Sunday School teacher's favourite and I *hated* it.'

'It seems to have worked,' Mae said. She liked the hymn and felt braver for singing it.

'Let's see how far we can get with Ginsberg's "America",' Eden said, wiping a bead of sweat from her forehead. 'We should be able to recite the whole thing the length of time we spent on it at school. What comes after line six? Is it "I won't write my poem till I'm in my right mind" or "until I'm right in my head"?'

They argued and added lines, altering them, forgetting, remembering. From Ginsberg they moved on to Sylvia Plath and Etheridge Knight. Darkness closed in around St Michel. A documentary took over from a quiz show on the television. Mae replaced a Diana Ross tape with a Marti Webb tape and put on an LP of modern jazz.

Gussie was oblivious to the noise, her eyes fixed firmly on the clock. Eleven o'clock; eleven fifteen.

'*Augusta.*' Like waves pounding ceaselessly on a beach his voice permeated her mind. She began to sing loudly and disjointedly, marching up and down the room, determined to drive him away, not to be seduced by the dark timbre of his voice.

At eleven thirty-five Eden said unwillingly, 'It's time we went upstairs.'

'Can't we do it down here?' Mae asked pleadingly.

Eden shook her head. 'No. It must be done just as your grandmother said. Are you ready, Gussie?'

Gussie gazed helplessly around the brightly-lit kitchen. Perhaps if she closed her senses to it, took sleeping tablets, the nightmare would go away.

'*Augusta.*' The voice battered to get in through the door of her mind. There could be no escape. Only confrontation would set her free. With leaden footsteps she followed Eden up the sweeping curve of the stairs and into her bedroom. It was just as it had been a year ago. Her score of dolls sat unblinkingly on the patchwork-covered sofa. The muslin drapes and netting on her four-poster bed were looped and tied with bows of blue ribbon. Candles stood in ornate silver holders on either side of her dressing-table mirror.

'It's eleven forty-five,' Eden said quietly, her heart beginning to race.

The blood had drained from Gussie's face. 'I must change. I must wear my wedding gown.'

'Oh, but . . .' Mae began.

Eden silenced her. 'I don't want you to say another word, Mae. I want you to sit in utter silence. If we need help I will yell to you, and whatever I yell, you do, *immediately*. Understand?'

Mae nodded and sank back into the sofa, clutching hold of the crucifix at her throat.

Eden slid the lace wedding dress over Gussie's head and shoulders, fastening the pearl buttons at the wrists, flouncing the skirt out with a trembling hand.

'What now, Gussie?'

Gussie licked dry lips. 'The candles. I must light the candles and turn off the lights.'

Mae whimpered protestingly and lapsed into silence. Gussie's eyes held Eden's. 'Whatever happens tonight, I want to thank you both for caring enough to stay with me.'

Eden's throat tightened. 'Don't talk as if you're going to die, Gussie. You'll be able to thank us afterwards.'

Gussie's eyes were unconvinced as she turned away from her friends and set needles and writing paper on the polished surface of the dressing table. Unable to do any more, Eden withdrew to the bed and curled up against the pillows, her heart slamming painfully and irregularly.

Slowly Gussie lit the candles and stared at her reflection

in the glass. A year ago she had sat thus, happy and carefree, certain of her heart's desire. With a heavy hand she picked up her silver-backed hairbrush and began to brush her hair so that it fell around her shoulders and down her back in a golden sheen.

Eden watched the second hand of her watch creep round once; twice. It was five to midnight.

The air seemed to have been sucked from the room. Gussie continued to brush her hair rhythmically. Waiting. Another minute; and another. The walls of the room seemed to be moving in on her. There were tight bands of steel around her chest, squeezing and tightening.

'*Augusta!*' The voice was loud and clear, menacingly confident. '*I'm coming for you, Augusta. We're going to be together forever and forever . . .*'

Behind her in the mirror she saw Eden nod her head. The fingers of her watch stood at twelve midnight. Mae pressed her hand against her mouth. Eden offered up a silent prayer. Gussie laid down the hairbrush and picked up a long needle. For one brief, terrible moment she hesitated and then she plunged the needle deep into the wedding finger of her left hand. The blood sprang in clear, scarlet droplets, scattering on to the virgin-white of the lace, spreading and staining. Dipping her mother's pen into the blood, she wrote her own name and that of Beau's on the paper in front of her.

The letters were disjointed and uncontrolled, like those of a child learning to write. 'Augusta Lafayette. Beauregard Clay.' With dark, terrified eyes she raised her head from her task and stared into the candle-lit mirror. The room seemed full of smoke. She could no longer see Eden's shadowy figure; no longer see the sofa and the dolls and Mae; no longer see even the walls. Only her face, white and ravaged, bearing little resemblance to the face that had once been hers.

The soft footfall on the gravel was unmistakeable. It came

again, nearer and nearer. Unhesitating and purposeful. For a crucifying moment, an aeon, there was silence and then the knocker fell hard against the wood of the door.

Gussie closed her eyes, fighting the battle that only she could fight. The knocker slammed hard again, reverberating through the now still rooms. She opened her eyes, staring sightlessly into the glass.

'Please go and open the door, Eden.'

Eden stared at her, paralysed by fear. The knocker fell again.

'He must be let in, Eden.'

Fearfully Eden swung her legs to the floor and stumbled towards the door and staircase. Through the slanting glass panels of the great front door a shadow loomed. Tall and broad-shouldered, unleashed power emanating from it in waves.

'Holy Mary, Mother of God,' Eden whispered, her blood turning to ice as she forced herself forward. 'Pray for us sinners, now and at the hour of our death . . .'

The knocker fell again. In the darkness of the hall Eden's shaking fingers closed over the latch. He was there, only inches away from her, separated only by glass and wood. Sweat rolled from her forehead and into her eyes. It should have been Gussie at the door; Gussie enduring the horror of opening it to the presence outside. No. Gussie had to remain upstairs. Had to finish the ceremony she had begun. If Gussie opened the door to Beau she would be lost. And, if she herself opened the door . . .

Her fingers closed around the cold metal of the latch. 'Oh Jesus, God,' she said, and released the lock. The door handle turned easily and smoothly. Her blood turned to water and then the door was opening and she shielded her face in terror as an ice-cold blast blew in from the hot, sultry night, searing her skin and robbing her of breath. She tried to scream as

189

it passed her by but no sound would come from her frozen throat. Helpless, her heart poised on the edge of death, she slid against the wall and fell in a crumpled heap to the freezing marble floor.

Gussie heard the opening of the door; felt the cold gust of air that snaked up the stairs and into the room. With dark, tragic eyes she reached for the piece of paper and held it high in her hand. This was the moment she had waited for; the moment when Beau Clay would enter her room and claim her as his love forever and eternity.

'*Augusta!*'

She stared steadfastly into the glass.

'*Augusta!*' His breath was on her cheeks. The candle flame spluttered and waned and then flared once more. He stood behind her, so near that she had only to turn in order to touch him. Not an image. Not a figment of her imagination. Real and tangible. Filling the room with his masculinity.

'*Augusta . . .*'

He was moving towards her, his lean, dark face as handsome as it had been in life. His eyes brilliant with triumph.

'*Augusta . . .*'

Above the candle flame the paper wavered. Desire flooded through her like a spring tide. She could turn, step towards him, be united with him in death forever . . .

'Oh my love,' she whispered brokenly. 'I'm sorry. So sorry . . .'

The paper dipped into the flame, caught and flared.

The triumph in his eyes turned to shock. Vainly he tried to reach her and touch her and failed. The paper blazed. In the darkness behind her he was no longer so clearly defined. His figure was blurred with the shadows and the smoke, his face hovered in the glass, black eyes imploring, beseeching.

'Goodbye, sweet love,' she whispered and then the flame burnt her fingers and the smoke-black paper tumbled into ashes, falling in a rain of white-hot dust. Behind her, the face that had been so confident, so insolently self-assured spiralled into the eternities. Only shadows remained. She could see Mae, huddled on the sofa, transfixed with terror. The dolls, neatly arranged; the bed, virginal in its heavy lace canopy. There was no Beau. He had gone from her life as she had desired him to. Forever. She raised her hands to her face and began to weep.

Deep in Cajun country, in a small forest clearing, a petite figure lay huddled. The face was old, with no vestige of the beauty it had once possessed. A travesty of a wedding dress hung on the bird-like bones, the cheap lace yellowed and mildewed. The hands were spread out on the beaten earth, fingers clawed in death. A little way away, half-hidden by a clump of wild lilies, gleamed the tarnished silver of a ring. A ring that had been defiantly ripped off only seconds before death. A ring that had kept its owner implacably bound throughout life. A ring in the form of a serpent.

On a distant highway, ten miles east of Houston, Bradley Hampton felt as if a physical weight had been lifted from his shoulders. It was crazy driving through the night to reach Gussie when she had kept him at arm's length for so long. Nevertheless he felt an overpowering compulsion to do so. He had waited long enough. He could not be expected to wait forever. He flicked on the car radio and began to whistle as the Thunderbird sped out of Texas and towards Louisiana.